FOREVER ONLY ONCE

A Promise Me Novel

CARRIE ANN RYAN

FOREVER ONLY ONCE

A PROMISE ME NOVEL

By
Carrie Ann Ryan

Forever Only Once
A Promise Me Novel
By: Carrie Ann Ryan
© 2020 Carrie Ann Ryan
ISBN: 978-1-947007-85-7
Cover Art by Sween N Spicy Designs
Photograph by Wander Photography

Praise for Carrie Ann Ryan

"Count on Carrie Ann Ryan for emotional, sexy, character driven stories that capture your heart!" – Carly Phillips, NY Times bestselling author

"Carrie Ann Ryan's romances are my newest addiction! The emotion in her books captures me from the very beginning. The hope and healing hold me close until the end. These love stories will simply sweep you away." ~ NYT Bestselling Author Deveny Perry

"Carrie Ann Ryan writes the perfect balance of sweet and heat ensuring every story feeds the soul." - Audrey Carlan, #1 New York Times Bestselling Author

"Carrie Ann Ryan never fails to draw readers in with passion, raw sensuality, and characters that pop off the page. Any book by Carrie Ann is an absolute treat." – New York Times Bestselling Author J. Kenner

"Carrie Ann Ryan knows how to pull your heartstrings and make your pulse pound! Her wonderful Redwood Pack series will draw you in and keep you reading long into the night. I can't wait to see what comes next with the new generation, the Talons. Keep them coming, Carrie Ann!" –Lara Adrian, New York Times bestselling author of CRAVE THE NIGHT

"With snarky humor, sizzling love scenes, and brilliant, imaginative worldbuilding, The Dante's Circle series reads as if Carrie Ann Ryan peeked at my personal wish list!" – NYT Bestselling Author, Larissa Ione

"Carrie Ann Ryan writes sexy shifters in a world full of passionate happily-ever-afters." – *New York Times* Bestselling Author Vivian Arend

"Carrie Ann's books are sexy with characters you can't help but love from page one. They are heat and heart blended to perfection." *New York Times* Bestselling Author Jayne Rylon

Carrie Ann Ryan's books are wickedly funny and deliciously hot, with plenty of twists to keep you guessing. They'll keep you up all night!" USA Today Bestselling Author Cari Quinn

"Once again, Carrie Ann Ryan knocks the Dante's Circle series out of the park. The queen of hot, sexy, enthralling paranormal romance, Carrie Ann is an author not to miss!" *New York Times* bestselling Author Marie Harte

To R, S, & K.
Thanks for taking this ride with me.

Acknowledgments

This book started off as a fun way to make a date and ended up with fun tagline of "it starts with a blind date and ends with murder."

That is all thanks to Nana Malone.

These characters weren't my romcom and Nana knew it. So thank you for never letting me take my foot of the gas in this book.

A huge thank you to Chelle for wrangling my words and asking the tough questions. And next time, call me. You know we are horrible at emails when it comes to this job between us LOL.

Thank you Jaycee for this cover. I GASPED when I first saw it and cried. You figured out what I wanted before I did. So thank you!

And thank you to Wander for this image! They are the perfect Cross and Hazel!

And as always, thank you dear readers for going on this journey with me. I hope you love the Brady Brothers and the PROMISE ME series!

Happy reading, everyone!

~Carrie Ann

Forever Only Once

From New York Times and USA Today bestselling author Carrie Ann Ryan comes a sexy new contemporary stand-alone series.

Hazel Noble has survived horrors she wouldn't inflict on her worst enemy. Since then, she's healed, found herself, and connected with a group of women she's proud to call her friends. However, when they make a pact to start looking for love, Hazel finds herself not only up first but also forced to face a past she thought she'd escaped.

Cross Brady has no need for a relationship. As the oldest of five, he's always been the one his family can rely on. Now, all he wants is to work in peace and live his life. His priorities shift dramatically, though, when Cross finds himself in Hazel's path.

Though the two initially fight their connection, they soon learn that it's safer to fall for each other than keep running from what's holding them back—not to mention, who wants them dead.

Chapter 1

Hazel

I COULDN'T AFFORD TO BE LATE TODAY. I HAD promised that I would be there on time because everybody else had meetings and other appointments after our coffee break, and I couldn't be the one to hold them back. It didn't help that I had hit every single red light on the way here, and a student had come in to ask a question just as I was about to head to my car. I'd stayed later than I wanted to, mostly because I would never leave a student hanging. He'd had legit questions, and even though my office hours had run an extra thirty minutes past my scheduled time, I felt like I had helped him solve a few problems so he could work on the rest on his own. Thankfully, that student was also one who asked pointed questions, which got him thinking.

That didn't always happen with some of my students at UB.

Even though I truly loved them and was glad to help, doing so meant I was now running late.

I hated being late.

I crossed the street, moving away from the public parking lot, annoyed that I hadn't been able to find a spot in front of Dakota's café, the Boulder Bean.

I loved living in Boulder, the college-town feel with the central university taking up most of downtown, and my smaller university residing in a little corner. Boulder was weird, at least that's what everybody said. I kind of agreed. But after trying to find a place that called to me, I had needed weird, needed a little bit of home.

I didn't have any family left. Didn't have a place to call home outside of this. Boulder was it.

I loved my new city, though it wasn't entirely *new* anymore, seeing as I'd been here for long enough. I'd made friends, ones that I truly liked. An inner circle that was waiting for me because I couldn't find a fricking place to park. Parking was nearly always a nightmare.

Boulder had boomed over time, and it was getting a

little ridiculous now. I found it harder to find my little piece of privacy and peace.

Tourism was getting more substantial thanks to the fact that I lived in one of the most beautiful places in the world. The mountains were right behind me, the foothills gorgeous and looking as if they were painted on the horizon.

I tried to take pictures, but it just didn't work out. A photo could never capture the true beauty.

I loved Boulder. I loved the home that I had been forced to make for myself. I did not enjoy the fact that everybody and their mother was moving to Boulder. I might technically be a transplant, but I liked to think of this as my new home. If I had my way, everyone else would just stay away for a minute so I could enjoy it. I knew I was part of the problem—I hadn't been born here, after all—but I wasn't going to think too hard on that.

I took another turn and ran straight into a massive chest.

I held back a curse, mostly because I hadn't been watching where I was going, just like he clearly hadn't. He gripped my elbows, clutching them ever so slightly. My heart raced at the unwanted and unexpected contact, and I froze, every single lesson I had learned in my self-defense classes seeping out of my mind as I tried to catch my breath. I grabbed onto my purse strap, as if that could protect me. Then I looked up—and up—at the man in front of me.

He was clean-shaven, wearing a perfect suit, his thin tie finished with an elegantly crafted knot at the neck. He smiled down at me, his eyes full of warmth...and something else I didn't want to name.

I had gotten skilled at deducing what a man thought when he looked at me.

I didn't like what I saw with this stranger.

"Hello there," he said, his voice deep, a little accented. Irish, maybe? That didn't sound right, though. No, it sounded as if he had been watching a little too much British TV and decided to add an accent to his voice.

With his hands still on me, seemingly not willing to let go, my heart raced, and flashes of other hands came at me, shaking me to my core. But these weren't those hands. This was not *him*. I needed to remember that.

"Sorry," I said, annoyed with myself for even apologizing since we'd both been in the wrong and moving too quickly. But I had run into this stranger just like he had run into me, so perhaps I'd needed to apologize anyway.

"No need to be. It's good to have...run into you."

I attempted to move away, but he kept his hands on me as if he were trying to keep me steady.

I tried not to let the bile make its way up my throat.

"Excuse me. I need to go."

"I just want to make sure I didn't hurt you. After all, we did hit kind of hard. This will be a funny story we can tell our children one day. Don't you think?" He winked, and I just blinked at him.

Was that supposed to be a line? One where he still wouldn't let go of me?

I took a deep breath and twisted in his arms so he *had* to move his wrist or risk it getting broken.

He took a step back and frowned at me.

"What the fuck?"

My pulse pounded in my ears. "Thanks for making sure I didn't fall, but I'm fine now. Have a good day."

I moved a step forward to get past him, but he gripped my arm again.

"I was only making sure you were okay. There's no need to get hostile. I'm safe. I'm not one of *those* guys."

"Sure. Have a good day." I moved forward again. This time, his other hand reached down and grabbed my ass.

I froze and turned toward him.

"Are you serious right now?" I asked, my heart racing, a lump in my throat.

"If you're going to treat me like a lecher, I might as well get something out of it." He narrowed his eyes. "Bitch." And then he pushed ever so slightly, and I wobbled on my heels before he turned and walked away.

No one noticed the interaction, everyone was too busy with their phones and their own lives.

No one had seen that he'd assaulted me, called me a bitch, and almost hadn't let me go. If I hadn't known how to get out of that hold, I wasn't sure he would have let me go at all.

My lips were dry, and I knew I was sweating. I took a deep breath and practically ran towards the café, hoping my friends were already there since I was running late as it was.

Despite hoping they'd beat me to the café, I also needed a moment to collect myself. The others didn't need to see me like this.

No one did.

They might understand because they knew my past, at least most of it, but I didn't want to talk about it.

I wanted to forget every memory, every moment of pain, everything about that time. I didn't need to bring it up again, even with the women I counted as family.

I nodded at a few people and pasted a smile on my face that I knew probably looked a little manic. Regardless, they smiled back. Boulder people were quite friendly if you tried.

I quickly made my way to the front of the Boulder Bean, a cute little shop with coffee brands listed in the windows, and a small coffee mug with steam billowing off the top as the café's logo.

I let out a breath, rolling my shoulders back and telling myself that nothing was wrong. That everything was normal. Then, I walked inside.

There were tables strewn about, and a couple of booths with comfy seats along the walls.

Some people were working on their laptops, others looking at their phones or just sitting down and enjoying a cup of coffee. A couple of students worked with textbooks and notebooks in front of them, their laptops closed so it looked like maybe they were doing math. They weren't my students, but I almost wanted to go over and see what they were working on.

I was a math professor. It soothed me to work with numbers, especially when I sometimes didn't feel soothed at all.

I looked to the back corner, in the booth nearest the front counter, and smiled at the three women sitting there.

Dakota, the owner of the Boulder Bean and my friend, got up and walked over, her eyes narrowed as she looked at me.

I knew Dakota had come from a life far different than mine. Though our paths had crossed thanks to an incident that mirrored what'd happened to me, we didn't talk about that.

We did our best to forget our pasts, all of us, and I was fine with that.

We were friends because we wanted to be, not because we wanted to share our deepest and darkest secrets.

"Hey, I was just about to call you. Are you okay?" Dakota asked, reaching out and hugging me. I hugged her back and inhaled her scent. She smelled of cinnamon, coffee beans, and vanilla today.

The Boulder Bean was mostly a coffee shop, with just about any kind of coffee arrangement you could imagine. But they also did decent business with tea, mainly because Dakota loved tea, but coffee was her bread and butter.

They had a few snacks as well, things that Dakota made in the back, or ordered in from a small shop nearby. But she did her best to make the Bean a pure coffee shop, mostly because there were enough cafes around the area and she wanted to stand out just a little bit.

"Sorry, I ran behind at work. I apologize for being late."

Dakota narrowed her eyes. "You're all clammy and pale. What happened?"

I just smiled. "Good to know I look like crap."

"Stop being evasive," Paris said as she slid out of the booth, Myra right behind her.

The four of us had become friends a couple of years ago, though I had met Paris in college and knew Myra from when we were younger. Our families lived near each other, and with the way our families were, that meant we were always forced to attend the same parties and the same high-society events.

It wasn't my favorite thing. However, Myra and I had been close, even though we'd been a couple of years apart in school.

Paris had been in a few classes with me in college. And Dakota owned this coffee shop. When I came in with Paris one day to catch up, we had started up a conversation with Dakota, and everything had snowballed from there. When Myra moved back to town, we picked up our friendship right away, and now it was the four of us against the world.

At least, that's what we told ourselves.

"Let me get some coffee, and I'll explain it all."

"What are you in the mood for today?" Dakota asked, taking a step back so both Paris and Myra could hug me.

I embraced them tightly, closing my eyes for just a minute so I could pretend that I wasn't still shaken or on the verge of throwing up.

"I'd love a vanilla latte."

"That's easy. I can do that for you. Now, go sit down.

We already have a plate of pastries because...why don't we just attack ourselves with sugar?"

I smiled at Dakota as she walked off and then followed Paris and Myra to our booth. We didn't always sit here, but it was the most convenient booth for us to use when Dakota still needed to work.

And while Dakota's staff was on the clock, and Dakota technically didn't need to be behind the counter today, I knew that my friend wanted to make our coffees herself.

Her staff didn't mind, at least that's what they'd told me. They knew that Dakota was just particular when it came to her friends and her family.

Not that Dakota had much in the way of family, but the other woman was just as secretive as the rest of us.

"You want to tell us what happened?" Paris asked, raising a brow.

"Let's wait until Dakota's back," I said, knowing that I wouldn't get out of this. Frankly, I just wanted to get it off my chest. What had happened outside wasn't why we were here today, so I'd just have to get over that little incident. It wasn't as if something like that hadn't happened before in my life. I held back a shudder. Sadly, it had. And incidents like it happened all over the world on a daily basis. Women were never safe. Not really.

Wasn't *that* a thought I wanted to think right then? I sighed.

"I have your latte for you. Now, tell us what happened," Dakota said as she took a seat in the booth. She had her back to the wall, her usual position so she could look out over her café.

I took a deep breath and tried to sound as nonchalant as possible, even though I was anything but. "Oh, I was just accosted on the road. I'm fine, though." Everyone started talking at once, and I held up both hands. "One second." I lifted the ceramic mug, blew on the top, and took a sip. I groaned, closing my eyes with my head tilted back. "Seriously, best coffee ever."

Dakota leaned forward. "Thank you. Now, go back to the whole thing you just said about being accosted."

I went through what had happened, and Paris's eyes narrowed into slits by the end of my story. She was already trying to push Dakota out of the booth as if she could find the man and attack him, but I held up my hands again.

"It's fine. Seriously. Let's just move past it. I'm not going to press charges, even if I ever see him again. It was just something that happened."

"It shouldn't have happened at all," Myra stated.

"But we both know it does. It's fine. I'll never see him again. If I do, I'll probably kick him in the nuts."

"You *should* have fucking kicked him in the nuts

today," Paris said, her voice low since she didn't want to curse in the middle of the café.

Dakota was the one who scared me, though. She just kept looking at me, her gaze intense.

"No harm done. I'm just fine," I said.

Dakota tilted her head, studying my face. "You are. If you weren't, we would go out and find that man, and we would cut off his dick." She smiled as she said it, but I froze for a second before everyone burst out laughing.

"You know it's always the quiet and sweet ones," Myra said, sipping her tea.

"I'm not sweet, and we both know it. I can't raise a little boy as a single mother and be sweet."

"No, I guess you can't," I said and then rubbed my temples. "Enough about me. We came here to talk about our plan. However, I almost feel like, after today, maybe I shouldn't join in."

"No, none of us is going to back out."

Paris pulled out her day planner and looked at the notes she had made before. "We are going to finalize this plan. Because dating sucks, online dating is worse, and the entire population of men has dwindled to like four single guys. *We* need to find them."

"I hope there's at least four," Myra responded, tapping her spoon on the napkin in front of her. "If there isn't, then we're going to have to share. And while I admire triads, I'm not the sharing type," Myra said, and I burst out laughing. It felt good to smile and laugh, and these girls usually did it for me.

"So the plan..." Paris continued.

"The plan," Dakota echoed.

"The plan is, we are going to find each other dates," Paris said sternly.

"Blind dates suck, though," I said.

"Have you ever been on a blind date?" Paris asked.

"No, but that doesn't mean they don't suck. Going out on a date is scary enough. Going out with a stranger?"

"A stranger that we will find for you. There are men in our lives at work, at the gym, at the grocery store, everywhere. A lot are kind. We've all said this in the past. But they just don't fit us for one reason or another. We're going to somehow make this work and happen for the rest of us."

"So...blind dates. That's what we're going with?" I was already nervous, and after what had just happened outside, I wasn't sure I really wanted to be part of this anymore. But it had been far too long since I had been on a date, and I missed it. Oh, I might still have some fears, but I missed being in a relationship. I missed being held. Hell, I missed sex, but that wasn't something I was going to say aloud.

"Not just blind dates," Myra corrected. "Perhaps

there's someone you already know in your life that we feel would be good for you."

"What do you mean?" I asked cautiously.

"We've already talked about this," Dakota said. "We're going to be open to dating. If there's a man in one of our lives that we feel would be a good fit for one of the others, that's one mark. Or maybe we want to help push each other in the correct direction." Dakota frowned. "Not...correct, but at least decent. You know, or just find something that actively promotes a healthy relationship." Dakota kept stirring her coffee. I wasn't even sure the other woman had taken a sip yet.

"Yes, healthy, loving, and hot relationships," Paris said, tapping her notes. "We've already discussed this. Today, we are here to go over the final rules and to draw straws."

"Do we need rules?" I asked, a little worried now that this was all becoming real.

"You are a mathematician," Paris said. "You love rules."

"I know that, but I don't know if I want to bring math into my relationships," I said, laughing. I paused. "So math in a relationship does sound kind of hot, but I'm a nerd."

"I'm pretty sure we all are at this point, especially if

we are actively pursuing this type of plan," Myra said, her voice soothing and always a little classy.

"What do we do?"

"We are going to work as a group to find each of us a happily ever after," Dakota said, nodding. "Because we are four amazingly smart, strong, and beautiful women." She rushed the last word, and Paris snorted.

"You are gorgeous," Paris said. "Don't even start with the whole 'y'all are so pretty, and I'm just plain' nonsense that you sometimes do. You're fucking gorgeous, so just shut up."

I snorted and sipped my drink.

"For such a sweet woman, your mouth sometimes surprises me," I said.

Paris raised a single brow. "I don't think anyone has ever called me sweet," she said and then looked down at her notes again.

"We all need to write down the characteristics that we want in a man. Even though we've talked about this before, we are going to double-check. Then, we will draw straws and work on each of us one at a time. However, as we go through this, if we find someone that's perfect along the way, we will take that into consideration. So, are we ready?"

"I guess I don't have a choice," Hazel said, swallowing hard.

"Good," Paris said and looked down at her notes again. "Most of us want similar things, kind, caring. Some of us want beards, no beards. But that is just part of the appearance section and doesn't matter so much."

"I would like it if he's not a troll," Myra said and then laughed. "I'm kidding. I'm not that much of a bitch. *That* much."

"We need four perfectly sexy but sweet, caring, gentle, growly, productive men. They need to have jobs, they need to—hopefully—not have criminal records, though we can look into that on a case by case basis," Paris said with a nod.

Dakota laughed. "This means we're looking for four bearded unicorns, is that what I'm hearing?"

I snorted and just shook my head. "We can look at the attributes at some point, but I honestly don't think that's what we're going to end up with. As long as they're not sleazy, slovenly, or sedate, it'll work for me."

"We're going against the three Ss," Paris said, taking down more notes. "We will look for our bearded unicorns without the three Ss. Either way, we need to do something. Because I am *not* trying online dating again."

"I don't even know how you did it the first time," I said honestly.

"Desperate times and all that. I have actual straws.

Paper ones because we're not using plastic straws here," Paris said, holding up four.

"Thank you for that," Dakota said.

"No problem. I've cut them down to size, and they're all in my hands. We're each going to choose a straw. The shortest one goes first, and so on."

"Not the longest?" Myra asked, her voice pure sarcasm.

"We can make it whichever one *you* get goes first if you'd like," Paris said, her voice haughty.

"Let's draw."

I closed my eyes and reached out, taking a straw. I didn't want to see. The others all whispered, and I opened my eyes, knowing exactly what I would find. Because, why not?

"Hazel, it seems that you will be the first to find your bearded unicorn," Paris said, writing down the order.

I didn't even look at who would be next.

It didn't matter, because it was my turn. I was going to find my perfect happily ever after.

And, somehow, I did not want any part in that.

Not after today. Not after what'd happened before. But I promised myself that I would try, and here I was, trying.

We went through the rules a bit more, but after looking down at my small straw, I knew I needed to go home and think. The others seemed to agree, wanting to do the same for themselves, so we disbanded.

I was quiet in the car, not even listening to music on my way home, trying to imagine exactly what would happen over the next few weeks. Would I finally go on a date? Would I find that bearded unicorn as the girls had called him? Or would I try, fail, and then hopefully move on to the next phase of this plan?

The latter seemed more likely. Mostly because I didn't trust myself to actually do anything about what I thought I wanted.

I pushed those odd thoughts from my head as I pulled into my driveway and got out of the car.

The hairs on the back of my neck stood on end, and I looked around as I walked up, confused. No one was there. Thomas wasn't here. I was just thinking about him thanks to that encounter with the stranger and now I was feeling things that didn't make sense.

I didn't see anyone, so I pushed aside those worries for now. I quickly got into the house and double-locked the door behind me, my pulse racing.

I was fine. No one was here to scare me. I was only seeing ghosts, things that didn't exist.

I was fine.

And, eventually, I would go on a date, living up to the

promise I made after a single glass of wine. I felt the little spark of hope that I had tried to ignore for so long.

Maybe this would work out.

Or perhaps I would end up broken again.

Either way, I had to try.

Because I had given up for long enough.

Chapter 2

CROSS

I WAS NOT GOING TO HIT MY COWORKER IN THE FACE.

I was not going to strangle him.

No, I was going to breathe, get through my anger, and realize that without coffee—for either of us—the guy was just an asshole. And I needed to get over it.

"All I'm saying, Cross, is if you worked a little faster, we'd get through our schedule the way we planned to all along. I mean, I know you're all into your art and shit, but we could be making some good money here."

I pinched the bridge of my nose. "Chris, we went into

this business together. We know what we're doing. However, you telling me to put away what I've been doing for what...ten years now? More? No, that's not how this works." I paused. "That's not how it's *ever* worked, and I'm not quite sure why you're acting like that's suddenly changed."

"Again, all I'm saying is if you put aside that one project for just a little while and work on these sets that could be for a larger commission, we'd make some quick money."

"*Quick money* isn't the way things work, Chris. We both know that. Quick money isn't a thing. It's a scam. If I set aside the commission that I have, then I'll be disappointing my clients, and I'll be the asshole. My current project is for a big client, and they help with word of mouth. They always have."

"It's a minor client, and we both know it." Chris folded his arms over his chest.

I closed my eyes again, trying to breathe through my nose. I had a temper, we both knew it. Hell, my family made fun of me for it. But I was also the steady one. I blew quickly, but then the anger went away, and I was there, solid as an oak, the one that stood against time—and all that other shit my little sister said.

"Chris, if you want to do those commissions, do them. That's your side of the business anyway. Me? I'm not going to set aside someone that we've been working with for years, just to work with a new person who says they're going to pay double. Especially when it's not in writing."

"You never did have ambition," Chris grumbled and then stomped out of my workroom.

I leaned back in my seat, pissed off that I had let it come to this once again. The two of us had worked together for fourteen years or so. We'd met in college, with me getting a business degree while working with wood and art on the side. I'd wanted to take additional art classes, as well as design classes, but I had known, even then, that I wanted to own my own business. I just needed to figure out how the hell to do it. So, I'd gone with a business degree while immersing myself in art on the side because I'd wanted to be my own boss, not work for someone else. The only problem was that I'd become best friends with Chris. The now egotistical asshole who was trying to give me a fucking migraine.

Chris wasn't the same guy he'd been over a decade ago when we decided to open up *Chris Cross Furniture*.

It had been a cute name back in the day, my younger sister Arden having helped us figure it out.

However, the Chris of *Chris Cross* was an asshole. He hadn't always been that way, but over time, he had wanted more money for less work.

I understood that, at least a bit. Of course, it would be

nice if I could make millions or whatever Chris wanted and not have to work every day, but that wasn't how the world worked—and *Chris Cross* did good business.

We actually did excellent business, considering how the economy went up and down like a yo-yo these days. We made good money because we took care of our work and our clients. At least, we used to. Chris hadn't been doing as much recently, and because we worked on our own commissions, that meant Chris wasn't making as much money as he used to.

I was just grateful that when we'd drawn up our contracts, it stated we would only pay ourselves based on what we worked on, rather than paying the business and then splitting it 50/50. That had been Chris's idea back in the day because he had been making more money at the time. He'd been a rising star in sculpture, and I'd been learning alongside him.

I hadn't minded the way the contracts turned out, because I wanted to be paid for the work I did, rather than taking part of what Chris did and vice versa.

We'd gone into business together because it was cheaper to share a space and the overhead. Property costs back when we first started had been high. Now, they were outrageous. But thanks to savings and my plans, I could afford the place on my own if I needed to.

However, the plan we'd made wasn't working the way

it should these days. In fact, if anything, it only got on my nerves.

The idea that we were furniture makers in this day and age wasn't exactly the easiest for some people to understand. But I spent weeks to months on a project, hand-carving tables and art and chairs, anything I could create with my hands. At the moment, I was working on a table worth five thousand dollars. That's what we had quoted, anyway. Sometimes this client liked to pay more, though, especially if I added in more details.

I wasn't banking on that though because I wasn't about to take advantage of people like Chris wanted me to. I cursed under my breath and then shook my head before moving from my seat so I could take a break. I couldn't focus on what I needed to do if I was complaining about Chris in my mind for hours.

Chris was off in his little workshop, music blaring. I hoped he was working. He had a commission coming up, and not the one that everybody wanted that he was begging me to work on.

Considering that my name was on the door, as well, it would be unfortunate if Chris started to flake. I honestly didn't know if I could trust him.

That meant I needed to start thinking about what we were going to do about the fucking business.

I let out a sigh and then went behind the building so I

could walk off my anger. I didn't smoke, hadn't since I'd bummed one when I was a teen and had promptly thrown up afterwards. But right now, I wanted a cigarette. Needed to do something with my hands so I didn't punch the wall or some shit. My phone buzzed in my pocket, and I smiled as I looked down at the name on the readout.

Yep.

My sister seemed to know exactly what I was sometimes feeling. Considering that it had always been my job to make sure I knew what she felt when she needed to go to the hospital, or when she just needed an extra pair of hands, it was nice that it worked both ways.

I answered the phone and smiled. "Hey there."

"Hi, big brother. I'm just checking in on you because I know you said you had a massive project due and wouldn't be able to come over for dinner later."

"I was just taking my break. It's as if you're watching me." I paused, looking around. "You're not like actually watching me right now, are you? Like creepily?"

"Shush. *You're* the overprotective creeper."

"Ouch. Anyway, I know you and Liam have a project coming up, too." Liam was Arden's former-model husband, an author and therefore one of my sister's clients, and a decent guy. If he weren't, I'd have already beaten his ass. However, he worshiped the ground that

Arden walked on, and was a protective asshole just like I was. We got along.

"Yes, Liam's on deadline, and so am I. Thankfully, on different books. He's leaving on tour tomorrow, though."

"I remember. I'll be there to help you move those few things we talked about. Things get rough in the house when you're both working on the same series, then?" I asked.

Arden was a virtual assistant and book researcher. I wasn't exactly sure how it all worked. All I knew was that she made sure she got the history and research right for her authors. That way, there was always someone double-checking and keeping timelines and facts straight. I hadn't known it was a real job until she started making good money and could finally afford her health insurance. And the fact that my baby sister had lupus meant that she needed some fucking good health insurance.

"We tend to snipe at each other if we're working on the same project. But I'm working on a legal thriller, while he's working on the first book in a new series."

"A new series? That's a big thing," I said, actually interested. Liam was a *New York Times* bestselling author of a series that put out one book a year, each taking about that long to write. It took a shit ton of research and traveling to get it all done, and I honestly loved the books. Not that I let Liam know that all the time.

"We mentioned that, didn't we?" Arden asked.

"I just didn't realize it was this book."

"This isn't even a spinoff. It's a whole new start. It's a little daunting, and I know Liam's worried. But I'm sure he'll do great. His readers will follow him. Maybe he'll even get some new ones."

"I'm sure he'll be fine," I said, being truthful. "I should probably pre-order."

"You should. Because you're not getting anything free." She paused. "You know I'm kidding, right? Because you can get anything you want from us. Liam said you're welcome to shop his closet for any book you need."

"I'm not taking advantage of my baby sister."

"You're never taking advantage. We're family. And family that I like. So, you're welcome to have a book. Now, I called to check on you, but it seems we're just talking about Liam and me. I love that you constantly do that," she said. I didn't think she actually loved it.

"Doing fine, just on a break."

"Is your table giving you trouble?" she asked, no hint of irony in her voice. I was grateful for that. My family *got* my job, but not everyone else did.

"Not really. Mostly, it's Chris." I whispered the words, knowing that my partner likely wouldn't be able to hear, but I was still careful. I didn't want to start another fight.

"What are you going to do? You guys are fighting more than ever lately, and I don't even really like him anymore. I mean, he used to be a good guy. I don't know... he just gives me the creeps now."

I scowled. "What?"

"It's nothing. He and I don't talk, which is a good thing because he rubs me the wrong way. Not physically. I don't know. He just seems like an asshole, I guess. Which isn't the nicest thing to say about your business partner, but here we are."

"I feel you." I pinched the bridge of my nose. "I don't know what I'm going to do. But something needs to change soon. I mean, I wonder if I'm going to have to figure out a way to either get out of this business entirely, buy him out, or start a new one on my own. I don't know, it all sounds like a fucking hassle, and a shit ton of money I don't have."

"We'll find a way to help you if you need it," Arden said, and I scowled.

"I'm not taking money from my baby sister and her husband."

It didn't matter that Liam was a fucking millionaire, I wasn't going to take money from them.

"You have given up so much to help me throughout the years. So, don't even. And Liam and I were already talking about it, so it's not like I'm just throwing money at you without talking to my husband first."

Somehow, I scowled even harder. "You and Liam talked about this?"

"Of course, we did. We're worried about you and Chris. And I'm bringing it up at the worst possible moment because I can't just sit around hugging you and telling you that I love you. But, seriously, if it gets too bad and you can't work it out, then Liam and I will help. And then you can pay us back, because that's what you do, and we'll call it a day. We are family. We are always there for each other. You were always there for me. You don't need to worry or work with Chris if it's going to give you migraines or some crap."

I shook my head, though she couldn't see me. "Thank you for the offer. I don't know what I'm going to do." I paused. "But, thank you."

"Always. You're my favorite oldest brother."

"I love the fact that you probably have a saying for Prior, Macon, and Nate, too."

"Of course. Though yours and Nate's are the easiest because it's my favorite oldest brother and my favorite twin brother. It's when I have to add more qualifiers that the titles get a little long. But it's worth it."

"You're a dork. And I love you."

"I love you, too. Now, I need to get back to work. I figure you do, as well."

"Get some work done. Maybe tomorrow you can come for dinner."

"Let's try that."

We talked for a few minutes more and then we hung up. Once we'd disconnected, I looked down at my phone, wondering if I could just call it a day. It was nearing five anyway, and I wasn't going to get any work done with Chris in the building. And that was another reason I needed to rethink this partnership. I hated that I even had to contemplate it, but if I couldn't work, that meant I wasn't making money, and then I couldn't pay my bills. I might have a decent savings account, and I was good about my retirement, but...fuck, even with the money I made on my pieces being far more than I'd ever thought possible, I didn't want to be lazy and just rely on the fact that I'd had a few really fantastic years.

I put my phone into my pocket and headed back into the building so I could drop my things and head home. I'd work on a few sketches for a couple of upcoming projects I had, and maybe even get some work done in my studio at home. It wasn't as big as this one, and I didn't have all the necessary equipment there, but I could at least work on a few smaller pieces. I hated when I couldn't work when I had the notion to, and I loathed not working a full day, so I'd built the little workshop a couple of years ago.

Chris came out from his side of the building, his phone in his hand, and a scowl on his face. I braced myself, knowing I probably wouldn't like what the other man had to say. Yet another reason I needed to rethink this partnership.

"Oh, good, you're still here. I have a favor to ask."

I tensed. "What kind of favor?" I asked.

"Oh, nothing too crazy. I'm supposed to meet with a potential client at 59th, but I don't know if I'm going to be able to get there because I'm finally figuring out what I need to do to finish this other project. Do you think you can meet with her?"

I blanked. "You want me to meet your client at a fancy bar?"

"Well, yeah. We were going to try to get dinner, too. Nothing untoward. I promise."

Chris had already been married twice and went through women like crazy, but I didn't say anything along those lines. After all, I was probably adding my own layer of bias to how Chris made decisions these days.

"What is it we're talking about?"

"I'll email you the details. But thank you."

"I didn't say I'd do it."

"I need you to. I'm finally getting somewhere with this piece. And I have that other meeting later."

"Other meeting?" I asked.

Chris waved his hand in the air. "With those potential clients. The moneymakers?"

I closed my eyes and tried to count to ten. I only got to four before I exploded. Albeit rather calmly, but still not as patient as I wanted to be.

"You want me to go to a fucking meeting at a bar on late notice with a woman I don't know so you can go and meet with the people who want us to mass-produce shit?" I didn't know what part of that bothered me the most, but putting it all together was too much.

"Hey, it was just a question. I don't want to cancel. But if you can't go, then don't worry about it. I'll make do. I always do."

It was the put-upon tone that made me say what I did next. I should have just said no and walked away, but I didn't. Because, apparently, I was a glutton for punishment, and I didn't want to disappoint anyone.

"Fine, send me the information. I'll go. But this is it. We're going to talk soon, Chris. Because this isn't working." I wanted relief to pass through me at those words. Instead, I just felt dread.

A look flashed over Chris's face, and he smiled,

looking almost like the guy he used to be, but still not quite. It was that off part that worried me. "We can talk. But this is going to work. I promise. I'll send you all the specs. We'll get it done."

"But...a bar?" I asked.

"59th is good. And it looks like you could use a beer. Am I right?"

Chris laughed at his own joke, then waved and went back to his side of the building, closing the door behind him. I stood there, wondering what the fuck I was doing. Was I really going to a bar?

I looked down at my clothes and cursed. I needed to change if I wanted to look like I at least belonged there. I didn't need to go covered in wood shavings. I went back to my office, grateful that I had slacks and a button-down stored there. Sometimes, I got too into my work and ran late for dinners with the family. I didn't always have to dress up for them, but occasionally, we went out. So, I was lucky I had some clothes stashed.

I entered a note in my calendar to replace them, because if I didn't, I'd surely forget, and then I checked my email for the info from Chris.

The client wanted some type of art sculpture that was not in my repertoire. It was more along the lines of what Chris did. But I looked down and figured we could talk about it, as well as the pricing that Chris had set up. I winced, knowing that it would suck going over those specifics with the woman, but this was Chris, and we needed the money for the business.

I looked down at myself, figured I looked presentable, and then headed to my car to go to 59th.

59th was a martini and vodka bar downtown. It wasn't actually on 59th Street. Apparently, it was a sister bar to another one in a bigger city than Boulder, so they'd kept the name even without the matching street.

I had been there a couple of times, and they did have good drinks, if a bit overpriced.

Somehow, I found parking a block over, paid the ridiculous fee, and made my way to the establishment, knowing this was likely going to be a waste of time. I wasn't the artist she was looking for. Besides, I had no idea what she looked like other than, according to Chris, she was "a hot brunette with ample curves and a nice rack."

A sexual harassment suit waiting to happen that I would probably have to deal with if Chris ended up working with this woman.

I made my way inside and looked for a single woman with long, dark hair. I found one sitting alone at a high-top, looking down at her phone as if she were waiting for someone. She had long, brunette hair that fell down her back, a few strands over her shoulder. She wore a sexy green dress that seemed to wrap around and showcase her curves. She had on high heels that looked like they would make her trip, but I had a feeling she knew exactly how to walk in them. She seriously looked like sex and sin. Somehow, I both wanted her to be the right person and didn't.

But it had to be her, there wasn't another single woman in the place, and I was already running late. So, I made my way over to her and grinned.

"Hi, I think you're looking for me."

Her eyes widened, and she smiled and gestured at the seat across from her.

It took me a second to blink because of that smile, and then I sat down, letting out a sigh.

"Sorry, I'm late."

"No worries, I was actually a little early."

I looked at her then, my cock getting hard, the reaction pissing me the hell off. Yet I wondered how the hell I had never met this woman before, and why Chris had been the one to meet her first.

And then my phone buzzed, and I looked down and wanted to slam my head against the table at the same time I felt like laughing.

"What is it?" the woman asked.

"You're not Cassidy, are you?" I asked. Her eyes widened comically, and she shook her head. "No, I'm Hazel. You're not Stavros?"

I snorted. "Nope, I'm Cross. I do believe I have encroached on your date."

Turned out, Cassidy, the potential client, wasn't coming, after all. However, I now found myself not wanting to leave.

And that was a problem.

Chapter 3

Hazel

I LOOKED AT THE MAN WITH THE LONG BEARD, rumpled hair, thick thighs, and broad shoulders, taking in his woodsy scent that went straight to places that made me warm. I wanted to crawl under the table and pretend that none of this had happened.

Why hadn't I introduced myself right away? Why hadn't I asked if this was the right man?

I had been blown away by his smile and looks, and I was probably now sitting at a table with a serial killer. Great, so this was how I was going to die—the sheer stupidity of an accidental blind date.

Hell.

My phone buzzed at that moment, and I didn't bother to look down before reaching for it. I couldn't tear my gaze away from the man beside me. I answered it without even looking away from Cross, wondering what the hell I was going to do. How were we going to get out of this particular situation?

"Yes?" I said into the phone.

Paris began sputtering. "I am so sorry. I am a horrible person."

I shook myself out of my reverie and frowned, pulling my gaze from Cross's face. "What?"

"Stavros. He can't come. His daughter? The one I told you about? She needs an appendectomy. Like right now. He's in the emergency room and frantic and texting me to let me know that he can't make it. He feels horrible, and I'm sure we can reschedule, but his baby girl is getting her appendix out right now and is about to go under anesthesia for the first time. Obviously, he's freaking out, and currently in a fight with his ex-wife. Fun times."

Paris said that practically in one or two breaths, and I winced, trying to catch my own breath.

"Oh," I said.

Well, that sounded about right.

"I'm so sorry. We'll fix this. The way tonight is shaping up is not the best way to start our plan."

I just shook my head and then realized that she couldn't see me.

"Don't worry about it. If you talk to him again tonight, tell him that I hope his daughter heals quickly and that everything's okay." I wasn't going to touch on the fact that he and his ex-wife were fighting, because that was not something I wanted to get in the middle of. "I need to go, but I will talk to you later."

"Are you going to leave the bar? You can come over here. I'm not doing anything. Which is kind of the point of all of this, but I digress."

I held back a smile at Paris's words, knowing her self-deprecating side was wholly honest. As it was, I couldn't keep my gaze off the man in front of me.

One I shouldn't be staring at.

"No, I don't know what I'm going to do. But I should go."

Paris tried to say something else, but I cut her off and then hung up. Then, I looked across at the man who had sat down at the wrong table.

"Um..." I had no idea what to say.

Cross smiled, even though it looked sort of like a wince at the same time. "I heard part of that. So, your date had to cancel? And I assume it was a blind date if you didn't know I wasn't him."

"I want to slink away in sheer mortification right now,

but I'm not quite sure what I'm supposed to say. No, my date is not coming because there is actual surgery and blood involved. Unless that's just an elaborate excuse. Maybe Stavros saw me, said ugh, and then left."

"That's not the case," Cross said, and I snorted.

"That's quite nice of you to say, but you're a stranger sitting at the wrong table. And now I'm dateless. I really should order that vodka martini and then call it a night."

"If it helps, I sat here for a meeting that my business partner was supposed to attend but was put on my plate at the last minute. I just found out that the client isn't coming at all. So, yeah. That's why I didn't know who *you* were."

I sat there, confused, and so out of my depth.

"I'd say you should join me, but that would be weird, right?"

I had no idea why I'd said that.

Cross tilted his head and looked at me. When the waitress came and asked for his drink order, he looked up at her for a second and then directed his gaze back to me.

"I'd love a beer if you have any," Cross said.

"We have over two dozen on tap."

"A lager. You choose. And thank you."

The waitress went off, probably a little sad that Cross hadn't even truly looked at her. And then I wondered what the hell I was getting myself into.

"So, I take it you're staying?" I asked bravely.

"Why not? This is a fun new story, right?"

His words echoed the man's from the other day, and I swallowed hard. "Maybe."

"What did I say?" Cross asked, leaning forward.

"Nothing."

"No, tell me."

I didn't know why, but I continued. "I ran into a man on the street a couple of days ago, and he grabbed me. Said it was funny and could be a cute story that we could tell our children. And then he wouldn't let go, and it was a thing."

Cross's eyes narrowed and darkened. "Are you okay?" I nodded, rubbing my elbows. Cross's gaze moved to follow the action, and his jaw tightened even further. "You sure?" Cross asked, his voice careful.

"I am. He ran away after I threatened him. I probably should have actually hurt him, but I was a little stunned."

"I don't blame you. I'm sorry that happened. And I apologize for bringing it back to the forefront of your thoughts. I can go. Seriously. We can cancel that beer, or I can just drink it at the bar and then head home."

I leaned forward, shaking my head. I didn't want him to go. I didn't know why I didn't, but I was tired of being so scared to act all the time. I'd lived my life like that for far too long as it was.

"No. Seriously, I'm fine. And you know what, why not? We'll have a drink and maybe dinner so I can actually drive home after a whole glass full of vodka. We'll just pretend this isn't weird."

Cross grinned then, looking sexy as hell, and I wondered how exactly this had happened.

"You know what? After my day, why not?"

"Are you going to tell me about your day?"

Cross smiled. "I think I will."

I tried to pretend that his smile did nothing to me. After all, I was on a date with a man I didn't know. But was it really a date? Or simply a dinner between two strangers. Honestly, how different would this be from how it would have been with Stavros?

Stavros would have been a stranger, too, although Paris likely would have made sure she knew a little bit about him beforehand. In fact, I was pretty sure my friend had a dossier on the man, as well as any others that might end up in this blind date game we were playing.

So, I tried not to think about the way Cross smiled at me, or the way it heated my skin, made the hairs on the back of my neck rise, and made my stomach clench.

Because it was just a smile.

Even the devil had a pretty face.

And that devil could look at you, and you would never

know that he was lying. That he was danger and sin wrapped up in a pristine bundle of muscle and soft skin and a beard that made his face look just a touch dangerous.

I didn't believe in thinking of a smile as more than what it was—a way to lower defenses. But I wouldn't let that happen.

Today was just a random set of events that meant nothing. However, they had led me onto this new road where I was somehow at dinner with a nice man in a public place. And I was safe, at least as safe as I could be, knowing what was out there.

"What's going on in that mind of yours?" Cross asked, his voice low, almost a growl.

He sounded genuinely concerned, and I rolled my shoulders back, trying to pretend that I was whole and not shaking inside.

I was really good at pretending.

"Sorry, it's been an odd day, and it's ending quite bizarrely, as well. Don't you think?"

Cross nodded and then leaned back as the waitress came with our drinks.

"Would you like a few minutes to look at the menu?" the waitress asked, and Cross nodded again. "Yes, please, I haven't even opened it yet."

"No problem. Dinners sometimes last a little bit

longer here," the waitress said, winking. My eyes widened.

"That was a little bit brazen of her," I said after she'd walked away, and Cross laughed.

"It was, but I think this is a place where most people go on first dates, don't you think?"

I shook my head. "Maybe. My friend was the one who set it up."

"Your friend?" he asked, and I shook my head.

"First, you. You said you were going to tell me about your day."

He searched my face for a little bit longer, and I felt as if he could read every emotion, see everything that made me tick. I didn't like it. After all, I barely understood how I'd handled today, I didn't like the fact that someone else could read me better than I could read myself.

"As I mentioned, I was supposed to be here for a work meeting," Cross began, and I tilted my head.

"Here?" I asked, a little incredulous. What he'd said about the place was true. Meeting a client here seemed a bit strange.

Cross snorted and took a sip of his beer. "Nice," he said, setting down the glass.

"They have some of the best drinks here," I said, taking a sip of my own.

He tilted his head and looked at me with those

gorgeous eyes again. "Cheers. I guess I should have done that first. I'm not very good at this. Not that I know exactly what *this* is."

I laughed softly. "You're right about that. There's nothing normal about today." I clinked glasses with him, took another sip of my drink, though only a small one because I was planning to only have the one.

I set my glass down, then played with the stem.

"So. You and work?" I asked, wanting to get back on track with the previous subject so I could focus and not let my mind drift onto odd paths.

"Yes," he said, his eyes clouding a bit. I wondered what that meant. "The co-owner of my business set this up so he could meet with a client, and then forgot to tell me until I was already here that it was canceled."

"It sounds more like a date, though. Am I right? Here? That doesn't make a lot of sense."

"Chris doesn't make a lot of sense."

"Wait, you own a business with a man named Chris? And your name is Cross?" I could have rightly slapped myself because I wasn't a fan of making fun of names. I didn't even know why I'd said it.

He just smiled. "It helps with the name of our business. Chris Cross Furniture."

My eyebrows rose to the top of my forehead. "Really? I know of you guys. A couple of my friends have some of your pieces. They're tough to find and purchase. Wow, I'm sitting at a table with an artist." A really wealthy artist from what I had read in an article in *Forbes*. Chris and Cross weren't just furniture makers, they were artisans who were sought after by people from all over the world.

It had been a couple of years since I had heard anything about them, but they had been very up-and-coming the last time I had seen anything mentioned.

"Anyway, I was supposed to meet a potential new client here, but it was someone for him. What she wanted isn't the type of work I do."

"So, you guys select your clients?"

"We're pretty much separate entities who share the business. Back in the day when we first started, we needed to share. Now, we're moving in different directions." He frowned. "And I have no idea why I'm telling you all of this. I haven't even told my family that."

"Maybe because we are both sitting with a stranger accidentally? I guess it gives us both an air of mystery." We smiled at one another, and I relaxed again.

"So, what is it that you do?" Cross asked. "And then I'm going to ask you why you were here on a blind date, if you don't mind."

I winced. "Let's not talk about the latter subject. Maybe. Anyway, as to your first question, I'm a math professor at UB."

"Really?" he asked, and I scowled. "Why did you say it like that? Is it because I'm a woman?"

"No, not at all. It's because you're so young. Back when I was in college, all of my math professors were old men with beards and tweed jackets, wearing corduroy pants that didn't quite fit."

I laughed at the image, shaking my head. "A few of my professors were like that, too. There's a new way though, women in STEM and all that."

"Oh, I totally believe it. Half of my architecture classes were full of women back when I was in school. Some of the guys didn't like that. Because, apparently, architecture and math and all of that should be all men, at least according to them."

"You're literally preaching to the choir right now," I said, snorting.

"I guess I am. So, what do you teach?"

"This semester, I'm only teaching one course. It's entry-level calculus. It's mostly the students who need it on their transcripts to get into other programs. Out of everyone in my class, there's probably only one math major. I'm not teaching any grad courses right now, though, because I'm doing a research semester."

"That's amazing. I was really good at math, but once I got past a few of the theoretical concepts? It just wasn't my thing."

"You work with math every day. But then you also work with your hands. You'd probably be more on the applied side."

My gaze trailed down. I noticed the scars on his knuckles, and exactly how big his hands were, and I swallowed hard.

Or, apparently, four sips of my drink were enough for me.

Cross noticed the way my gaze fell, and he raised a brow but didn't smirk at me. Instead, he moved the conversation along. I still had no idea why I was sitting here with a man I didn't know.

"So, you were supposed to be on a blind date. Who was he?" Cross asked.

I shook my head. "Does it matter?"

"If you're going on another date with him, it could matter."

"Not another. He didn't make it to this one." Shame covered me, and I shook my head. "His daughter went in to get her appendix removed. That's an actual reason for him not to come. A good one. Not an excuse. Now I feel horrible for even commenting on it."

Cross reached out and gripped my hand slightly before letting go. My skin burned at the contact, and I wanted more. What was wrong with me? I didn't even know this man. This wasn't like me. Still, all I wanted to do was lean forward and touch him again.

I'd clearly lost my senses.

"Anyway, I am on a blind date because I wanted to be." I raised my chin. "Is that a problem?" I asked, knowing I sounded a little bit defensive. Fine, a lot defensive.

"Not a problem at all. And I'm not going to give you a line and ask what a pretty girl like you is doing on a blind date or any crap like that. Considering that it's been way too damn long since I've been on a date myself...I don't know. Maybe I'd be up for a blind date, too." He frowned. "No, not given who my brothers would pick. Maybe my sister."

I leaned forward, interested. "I will pass over the whole not dating for a while thing and ask about your family. How many brothers? And a sister?"

"I have three brothers and a baby sister."

His eyes warmed as he talked about them, especially his sister, and I smiled. "Let me guess. Your baby sister is not a baby anymore?"

Cross laughed, a deep chuckle that went straight through me and did horrible things to my hormones. "No, she's not a baby anymore. In fact, she has a husband and is all happy and in matrimonial bliss. She would probably be the only one I'd let set me up with someone, but then again, I'm not a hundred percent sure I'd trust her decision with those rose-colored glasses."

"It's always the married ones who want to set you up. They know *just* the person."

"And the person who set you up? Is she married?"

I shook my head. "No, she's not." I didn't really want to get into the whole date pact thing that my friends and I had come up with. It sounded a little silly outside of the four of us.

"Anyway, back to the family thing. I have three brothers, all younger, all pains in my ass. So, no, I don't think I'd want them to set me up."

"I can see that being a problem."

"Do you have any brothers or sisters?"

"No, I'm an only child." My stomach clutched again, but this time not from heat. "My parents died a few years ago. It's just me."

"I'm sorry about that."

"It's been a long time." Not long enough, but I didn't think it would ever truly be long enough.

"Anyway, I have a good group of friends out here. That's why I'm on a blind date."

"You keep dodging the subject, even though you're talking about it. I feel like there's more you have to say about this date of yours. I mean, we may never see each other again after this. What's so mysterious about it?"

I studied his face, the strong line of his jaw, that little bump on his nose from where I was sure he'd broken it before. I realized I wanted to tell him. What was wrong with me?

"It's not entirely my story to tell," I said, surprising myself with the words.

His eyes widened. "So, there's a story."

"My three friends and I decided that it was time for us to actually start dating again. Meaning, setting each other up on dates. We decided to push each other in the right direction. I'm not quite sure how it's going to go with the rest of them, but I drew the short straw."

"Why do I feel like you're talking about literal straws?"

"Because I am. Paper straws that were cut. I drew the short one. That meant I was the first to be set up. My friend Paris knew this guy named Stavros. She thought he'd be perfect for me." Cross tilted his head, studying my face. "However, I don't think it's going to work out. There seemed to be some tension with his ex-wife," I added at Cross's look.

He winced. "That's never a good thing to get in the middle of. But with so many people on so many different relationship tracks these days, sometimes, you can't avoid it."

My brows rose. "Have an ex-wife then, do you?"

He laughed and shook his head. "No, never got that far. But I dated a few women in the past who had ex-husbands that weren't really keen on having their exes out there finding someone new. I mean, I sort of get it. When you say your vows, you form a connection with someone. When that's suddenly gone, you're a different person. Not everybody knows how to walk away."

My skin chilled, but I did my best to keep the smile on my face, even as I sipped at my drink.

No, not everybody did understand how to walk away.

"I'm sorry to interrupt, I was just seeing if I could get you guys something to eat," the waitress said. I met Cross's gaze.

"It's up to you," he said, and I took a deep breath. Then, I leapt. Because that's what tonight was about, right? Taking a leap. "I've already looked at the menu. How about I order while you look?"

Cross nodded. "That sounds like a wonderful plan, Hazel."

I loved the sound of my name on his lips, and that worried me. I shouldn't love it. I wasn't going to see him again after tonight. Right?

We talked about our work and a little bit more about our families and friends. We talked about nothing of importance, and about sports. We talked about Stavros and the fact that I probably wouldn't go on a date with him. And then we ate and laughed. I didn't think I had ever laughed so hard in my life.

Cross reached out and brushed his fingers along mine every once in a while, and my breath caught every time, making me wonder exactly how this had happened.

This was a date that wasn't meant to be. I didn't even know this man. For all I knew, everything he said was a lie. Maybe he was a serial killer. And although the thought of that chilled me, knowing what I did about others, especially those from my past, I kept going. Maybe this was a mistake, perhaps I was being that woman in the horror film that got murdered later because she was an idiot. But I wanted to believe, just for a moment, that things could be worth it, even for the moment.

When the bill came, Cross reached for it at the same time I did, and I shook my head. "Down the middle?" I asked.

"Really? Sharing the bill?"

"It's a date that isn't a date. We might as well continue on that path."

"I can do that. However, I'm pretty sure this *was* a date, Hazel."

I blinked as I set my card down next to his.

Cross Brady. That was the name he had given me. Unless his ruse was completely elaborate, that hadn't been a lie.

"Maybe it was a date," I said softly.

"Maybe. And, because it's a date, can I ask for your number?" Cross asked, and I froze. "You want to talk to me again?"

"Why not?" Cross asked, shrugging as if it weren't a big deal. It really was. "Maybe this is nothing, but I had fun tonight. And like I said, it's been a while since I've been on a date, real or otherwise. Even accidental."

I smiled at that.

"What if it's a complete mistake? What if, after this, the shades are drawn, and the facade slips away?"

"Then it does. And maybe the magic won't be there. Or, maybe this is just a start?"

"That's a really good line," I said, still heated.

"It really is," he said with a laugh. "So, what do you say?" he asked, and I licked my lips, noticing the way his gaze followed the movement.

This was probably a horrible mistake. We likely would never talk to each other after this.

But then again, tonight had been a night of firsts and what-ifs.

So I smiled and reached for my phone.

Chapter 4

CROSS

"YOU WANT ME TO PUT IT WHERE?" I ASKED AND laughed as my sister raised a single brow, her mouth pursed, though I knew she held back a laugh.

"You honestly don't want me to answer that question, do you? Because if I do in the same fashion that any of our brothers would, well...I think it would be kind of a painful experience."

I shook my head, grumbling, though my lips twitched. "As lovely as that particular image is, this box isn't getting any lighter, darling."

"And I said I could handle it," she said, frowning.

"I'm sure you can. But you're just now able to not have to use the cane all the time. So, why don't you just let me be a little overprotective?"

"You can put the box in Liam's office," she said finally, sadness touching her expression for just a moment before she let it slip away.

I held back a curse, hating that I had been the one to put that look on her face, then went to her husband's office to set down the box of books.

I turned towards Arden, who stood in the doorway, her arms crossed over her chest.

"I'm sorry I hurt you with what I said."

Her brows rose, and she shook her head. "No, you didn't hurt me, not even a little. I'm just in a funk because Liam isn't here, and I'm not with him."

I opened my arms, and she settled against my chest, wrapping her arms around my waist. I rested my head on top of hers, sighing a bit as she sank into me. I didn't get these moments often these days. She wasn't my little sister anymore. She was now married—a Montgomery. And in this state where there were so many damn Montgomerys, that was a big deal.

She was not only happy, she was also married to a former world-famous model turned bestselling author. It had hurt me just a little to watch her walk down the aisle with our dad, watch him give her away. I had been happy as hell to see her marry Liam and become part of his family, but part of me had wanted to steal her and run away to make sure she was safe.

She was still my baby sister, and always would be. But now, if she got hurt, she went to Liam. She didn't come to me or our brothers or our parents anymore. It was weird how everything had changed, yet some things remained the same. I had no idea how I had gotten so melancholic recently.

I kissed the top of her head and squeezed her slightly, then laughed as Jasper stuck his nose between us, wanting pets. I moved away from Arden and went down to my knees, running my hands over the white Siberian Husky. Jasper lapped at my nose, and I laughed. "I do love you, boy."

"He has been in a very playful mood. I do believe he's excited because he doesn't have to take a B-A-T-H."

My brows rose. "Why exactly doesn't he have to take...that?" I asked, knowing that Jasper was notorious for hating baths, and Arden hated giving them.

"He had one before Liam left, and it was a couple of days early. I feel like he knows when it's his usual time. He gets all stressed."

I shook my head. "Considering that you have to spell the word, he probably does. This dog's smarter than most members of our family."

Arden rolled her eyes. "You're talking about the brothers, aren't you? Because I'm pretty sure that Prior and Macon could totally kick your ass."

"Not Nate?" I asked.

"Nate is my twin, and while I love him, he would probably trip on his way to hurting you."

"You may be right in that. But, still, that's kind of cruel."

"I'm only telling you what I told him to his face yesterday." She grinned.

I laughed, then reached out to hug my sister again before following her into the kitchen. "Speaking of, when are they heading over here for dinner?"

"How did you know I invited all of them here for dinner?"

"I didn't know for sure, but I *did* mention that I was coming over here to help you with a few things because Liam was out of town. So, I figured they would invite themselves over."

"You're right. In fact, Macon already dropped off a few groceries for us. That way, I don't have to go out and get extra potatoes."

I scowled. "Why didn't you tell me? I would have gotten you groceries."

"I'm a big girl, and there is such a thing as grocery delivery these days." She put her hands on her hips and glared at me. "I have lupus, Cross. I'm not dying. Get that out of your head."

I visibly flinched at the use of the word *dying* and swallowed hard. "I'll always worry. I can't help it. I'm going to be the overprotective asshole forever, and you'll just have to deal with it."

"And *you* will just have to deal with the fact that I can do some things on my own. I can go grocery shopping. I can bring in baked goods for the retirement home. I can take Jasper out on W-A-L-Ks. I can do all of that. I'm healthy. I take care of myself. And we both know that Liam doesn't let me do anything too strenuous." She winked. "Some things can be a little strenuous."

"I swear to God if you elaborate on that, I am walking right out this door." I squeezed my eyes shut.

"No, you're not."

I opened my lids. Saw her eyes dancing with laughter. "You really have to stop doing that. You know it freaks all of us out."

"Perhaps, but I enjoy it. Anyway, the guys will be over soon, and I think that's all I needed help with. Thank you again for coming. That box was just a little too heavy since the UPS man put it at the foot of the porch stairs."

"Your normal guy is Mike, right? He doesn't do that."

"Mike is on vacation," she said and sighed. "The fact that I know the name of my UPS driver and that I know that he's on vacation tells me I probably order too many things."

"No, it just means you're friendly." I paused. "And you probably order too many things."

"Anyway, enough about me and all of my needs. How about you? Anything interesting happen in the few days since we've chatted?"

"Not really," I said, going to the fridge for a glass of water. I used the pitcher to pour both of us glasses and then handed her one.

"Keeping me hydrated?" she asked, a single brow raised.

"Taking care of you. Can't really help it. Plus, you know that Liam texted me earlier to make sure you're keeping up with your water intake. You know you were dehydrated a few days ago."

"I swear, it's like I got married, and Liam connected with you guys to the point that even *his* brothers are starting to worry about me. Everything's multiplied."

"We can't help it. We worry about you."

"Enough of that. Tell me. How's work? How's Chris?" she asked the last part with a wince, and I sighed.

"I think I hate my partner," I said honestly.

"I've never really liked him. He was always a jerk. And he kept hitting on me."

I set the glass down and leaned forward. "Excuse me?

When the fuck did he hit on you? You said this before, sort of, and I missed what you said. But why the tone now?"

She gave me a look. "*Excuse me.* He's always done it. Haven't you noticed that he gets too close when we speak? Or that he slowly encroaches on any woman's presence. It's creepy."

My stomach fell, and I wanted to punch something. "How the fuck did I miss that?"

"Probably because, at first, he did it when you weren't watching. And then you were so busy cleaning up after him that I don't think you were able to watch. You haven't had any complaints about it from any of your female clients?"

I closed my eyes and counted to ten. "No. What the fuck? We could get sued."

"You might. Or maybe he isn't as creepy with other women as he is with me."

"I could seriously kick his ass for this."

"No, that's Liam's job." She paused. "Or my job. But I'm not in the mood to kick anyone's ass. I'll just send over one of the Montgomerys. Or my other brothers."

"You won't let me do it?" I asked.

"No, because you still have to work with him until you dissolve the partnership. Speaking of, is that really what you're going to do?"

"Fuck. I have to end it. I cannot work with him anymore."

"What else does he do, other than what I could be overreaching with?"

"You're not overreacting. If you feel uncomfortable with him at all—something you probably should have told me about before so I didn't put you in that situation, or maybe something I should have just noticed—then that's a big thing. As for what I'm going to do with Chris? I don't know. I don't know if he's going to make it easy for me to dissolve the business. Right now, I'm the one making the bigger deals."

"I thought he wanted to make more money with those weird deals of his?"

"True, he does, but he isn't in the studio as much lately. Maybe he's working at his home studio like I sometimes do, but I'm in the main place far more than he is. His pieces make good money when he sells them, but he's been focused on different kinds of commissions recently. Not what we started with."

"And you're sure he can't take any money from the business for himself?" she asked.

I nodded. "Yes. I work with our accountant monthly to go through our expenses. I know what goes into the business and what comes out. He literally can't take any of the money I make on commissions. It goes back into the building—any percentage that comes off our base price, that is. As long as he didn't fuck up any of the paperwork before he sent it in." That was something I would have to look into. Hell.

"That's good. At least you had the foresight to put that into your contracts."

"I shouldn't have worked with him at all. I fucked everything up."

"No, Chris is doing that. I just hope you can get out of it soon."

"I hope I can, too. I need to figure out exactly how to approach that. Because at first, I thought maybe I could find a way to work with him, only in just a different aspect. You know? Make it easier. But I don't think I can. Especially given that I want to kick his ass for daring to touch you."

"He's never actually touched me, but he does encroach on my space and is sometimes inappropriate in what he says. I'm sorry for bringing that up."

I shook my head and drank some more water. "Don't be sorry. I'm pissed that I didn't see it before. And leaving Chris has been in the back of my mind for a while now."

"Let's talk about something else. Something happier. Have you been on a date recently? I know it's been a while."

I froze, blinking. How the hell had she known? I hated

that she could read my fucking face even beneath the beard.

"Oh my God. You have. Tell me about it."

"How can I help you start dinner?" I asked, changing the subject. Not that she would let me.

"No, no. You went on a date? With who? Tell me. How did I not know this? I mean, I knew it had been a while, though none of the others really made fun of you about it. But tell me. Tell me more."

"It wasn't really a date." I frowned. "It didn't start out as a date, but I think it ended as one."

"You're going to have to explain that because I'm a little confused."

"I met someone. Thanks to Chris, actually."

Her brows shot up again. "Really? Chris? Am I not going to like this woman?"

"She doesn't actually know him."

"I'm confused again." I laughed and leaned against the counter. "So, Chris decided to force me to meet with a potential client down at 59th."

"That's where he meets his clients? What is he, a gigolo?"

I laughed. "I don't think there are actual gigolos or paid escorts there." I paused. "Not that I know of anyway."

"Wait, are you dating an escort?"

I held up my hands. "Let me finish."

"Then start talking. Because all I know right now is that I'm thinking of Chris as a gigolo, and it's making me want to vomit."

I groaned. "Thank you for that mental image," I said. "Anyway, I had to meet up with one of Chris's clients because my partner is a piece of shit, and then it turned out that she didn't even come."

"Really?"

"Either she canceled, or he did. I don't know. It wasn't my client, I had nothing to do with it. Anyway, I saw a single woman at a table and sat down, thinking it was Chris's contact."

Arden put both hands over her face. "You did not." She groaned.

"Yep, I did. Because I'm an idiot. However, it turned out well."

"Really?" she asked.

"At first she thought I was her blind date."

"Oh my God, that's like the perfect meet-cute." Her eyes widened. "Wait, did her date show up?"

"No. So, it was just me."

"What an asshole. He stood her up? Who backs out on a blind date?"

I shook my head quickly. "Apparently, his daughter was sick."

"Now I feel like an asshole."

"Maybe you should let me continue the story."

"Fine."

"Anyway, once we realized that we had both made a mistake, we just went with it. She was nice, we talked, got along, and I got her number for maybe another date."

"Seriously, that's such a meet-cute. What's her name?"

"Stop calling it a meet-cute. And her name is Hazel."

"Cross and Hazel. That's so sweet."

"If you start singing about sitting in a tree, I will have to force you to give Jasper a B-A-T-H."

"That's cruel. For both of us." She put her hand over her dog's head and petted him quickly. "We don't want to scar him for life."

I gave her a look. "Anyway, it was a weird situation that turned out kind of nice." I shrugged. "I don't know if I'm ever going to see her again. She has my number if she ever wants to call."

"You can't just leave her hanging, Cross. She's probably waiting on you."

"It hasn't even been twenty-four hours yet. I'll text her. Maybe. I don't know."

"Don't be an asshole."

"I'm not trying to be an asshole. It's more that I don't know if I want to date. I have enough issues with work.

Adding a relationship on top of that probably isn't the best thing."

"Chris is already hurting your creativity. He's hurting your work. Don't let him hurt your personal life, too."

"I don't know. Plus, she may have another date by the time I figure out what I want."

"What do you mean? With that same guy?"

"I don't know about that. But she has this whole blind date thing going on with her friends."

I explained the pact that Hazel made, feeling kind of bad that I was telling the story, but it was Arden. She wouldn't tell a soul. Plus, I needed to talk this out. I really didn't have anyone else to do that with. I could talk with Prior or Macon or Nate, but they had their own issues. Arden was the only one of us who was truly settled. She was our touchstone.

She'd always been that, even when her life had been chaotic.

"That's genius. I kind of envy that she has those kinds of friends."

I reached out and tucked her hair behind her ear. "You always have us. And you have a set of girlfriends now." Arden had lost some of her friends over time because of her disease, people who couldn't understand that sometimes she simply couldn't leave the house. That, at times, her illness was the number one priority in her life, even if she didn't want it to be.

She had a new group of friends though thanks to her husband, and that was a good thing for her. And for me. I didn't like my sister feeling alone.

However, it just made me think that I really only had my brothers, and now Liam and his family. Chris had been my only real friend outside of the family. I hadn't needed much else before.

Now, it seemed as if I was going to lose him, too.

"Anyway, you know she has three friends, and you have three brothers. We could make it work." She clapped her hands, and I held up mine. "No, not even a little. We're not hooking up our brothers with those women."

"Do you even know them?"

"No, and neither do you. Let's not tempt fate and make anything more complicated than it already is."

"Because you want to call and see her again? And having your brothers date those women would make things a little awkward?"

"You sure do like to reach, don't you?" I asked, laughing.

"It's what I do. And, really? You're smiling when you talk about her. You don't smile much these days. I think you should call her."

I frowned. "I don't know. I don't want to complicate her life."

"A relationship is all about working through complications, about finding layers. And, even though I'm your sister and this is gross, it doesn't have to be serious. You could use a little companionship."

I winced. "Let's not talk about that."

"What? You're a nice, healthy male. You're getting up there in age. Maybe it's time for you to find someone."

"Don't call me old. You may be my little sister, but I can still beat you."

"You could try. But I'm pretty sure the Montgomerys could take you."

"You're using your husband's family as a shield?"

"Every day that I need to. Plus, I use you guys as a shield against them. Jokingly, of course. No one would dare hurt me."

"You bet your ass, they wouldn't. And, anyway, I have no idea what the hell I'm going to do about Hazel. But I liked the night we had, and I did ask for her number."

"You're the one who asked? Don't be an asshole. Call her. Text her. Do something."

"I know, I know. I just left the bubble of whatever we had, and I felt the weight of what was going on with Chris. It screwed up my perceptions."

"Don't let that happen. Be better than that. You

smiled. I like you smiling. Call her. Go on another date. One that you actually plan this time. And remember, you already have the perfect meet-cute."

"Stop calling it that," I said and then looked down at my phone. I wondered what I should do.

I'd loved every single moment of sitting at that table with Hazel. And I wanted to know more about her.

Even if I wasn't sure that either of us was ready for what that could mean.

Chapter 5

HAZEL

"But I can't find X."

I shook my head at my student's words, but let a smile cross my face. This wasn't our first set of office hours, and we had a system going by now.

"You will. Let's do it together. All we need to do is find the pattern. That's what this part of math is. Honestly, any math. It's finding a pattern. And if you can remember the rules, sometimes, the pattern helps you find the solution a little faster. Other times, you have to work to see it."

"But I'm not good at patterns. I was never good at matching things or anything like that in school before."

I looked at Dustin, my freshman student, and wondered how many professors and teachers had told him that he wasn't good at math. That math was for some people, and he just wasn't it.

While I genuinely believed that not everybody needed to understand high-functioning math, I had to be honest. While it wasn't required for every single person, I also knew that I had to give every individual a chance. It was fine if they didn't understand every nuance on the first try. That's why we practiced. That was why my exams weren't the only things that weighted the grade.

Another professor who taught calculus only counted three exams as the students' grade. The professor had gotten into trouble for weighting an entire semester's worth of complicated calculus on one test. Therefore, he added two more tests to his schedule, each one harder than the last.

Students continually complained about it, but there wasn't much I could do. After all, that sometimes worked. They excelled at it and continued on in their academic and professional careers to do greatness.

For students like Dustin, that wasn't good for him. He'd had to withdraw last semester because of that professor, and now he was in my class. Although I didn't do those exams the same way, my class was still difficult.

"Now, Dustin, let's start where you're comfortable, and see where we can go from there. You say you have problems with patterns? Well then, let's find another way."

"But what if I never get this?" he grumbled.

"If you go into this thinking you won't, it might become a self-fulfilling prophecy. I'm not saying it'll be easy. And I'm not saying that it will make sense right away, but we're going to try."

Some did end up making sense. It took the full forty minutes of his appointment with me, but he finally got through his homework.

He was exhausted, and I was a little tired, as well. I had to wonder why he was going into pre-med since when he wasn't working on his homework, he spoke of writing, something he loved, and his hatred of math and science. But it wasn't my place to point that out, at least not yet. Further on into the semester, when I got to know him better, maybe I could bring it up and help him figure it out. After all, just because he wasn't good at calculus didn't mean he couldn't do everything else that was required for his degree.

Although, the sadness in his gaze hit me hard. I wanted him to do well. To succeed. And that was why I did these additional office hours with him—and a few of my other students.

After setting up our next appointment, I leaned back in my chair and settled my thoughts. I had regular office hours coming up later in the day, but this was a standing appointment between the two of us. I had that with a couple of other students, as well, and it sometimes seeped into my research time, but it was worth it.

Getting into college was a huge thing, and there was so much pressure put on these kids starting at age fourteen or so. Now, they were eighteen and nineteen years old, possibly on their own for the first time, and a lot of them didn't know how to study. They knew how to take tests, they knew how to pass high school, but studying in a collegiate setting wasn't a skill that a lot of people had.

They had to teach themselves all over again how to get it done because there weren't a lot of ways to learn otherwise. There were study groups, and there were helpful hints and classes along the way, but sometimes, it just didn't happen.

I wasn't someone who could change the system, I didn't have that power, but I could help where I could.

"Time to get work done," I whispered to myself as I pulled my salad out of my mini-fridge and then got to work on my research. The other part of my office was covered in whiteboards and had a high-tech computer so I could get my work done. But right now, I just needed to focus on my notebook and scarf down this salad.

Sadly, I'd forgotten the dressing at home, so it wasn't going to be that great. I hadn't really been on top of my game for the past couple of days, and I blamed my accidental blind date for that. Oh, I probably could have blamed something else like stress over work, or my students, but it was nothing like that.

No, it was the date.

Cross.

And the fact that he hadn't texted yet.

Or called.

Not that most people called these days, but it could happen. It just hadn't.

I didn't know why I had put so much hope in the idea that he would. I didn't even know him. Just because we had gotten along well didn't mean we would have anything more. It was just a one-off, a beautiful night that had started off on a very different trajectory.

I didn't know why I was so disappointed that he hadn't contacted me. I had his number, and I hadn't reached out either. It just felt weird. And that was my problem.

I'd already put myself out there by giving him my number. And yet he hadn't contacted me. It had to be for a reason. Once he got home, maybe he'd realized exactly what a huge mistake he'd made. Or perhaps he *was* a serial killer and now knew my phone number, along with my likes and dislikes, and was planning to chop me up into little bits later.

I cringed. I really needed to get those thoughts out of my head. They weren't healthy.

"Knock, knock," Paris said from the doorway. I jumped, dropping my fork onto my desk.

"You scared the crap out of me. Thankfully, I forgot my dressing, or this would have been a huge mess."

I laughed as I said it, cleaning up my strewn lettuce and carrots.

"Sorry, I thought you saw me. You were off in your own little world." Paris knelt down by my desk and handed me a cucumber slice.

"Thanks," I said, wincing.

"No problem. I was going to see if you wanted to get lunch since I was out for a business meeting all morning. I don't have to be back for a couple of hours. But it seems you already have your lovely lunch."

"I didn't know you were doing business meetings now," I said, ignoring the swipe at my lunch. She was right, after all.

"Not all the time. But we're on the hunt for someone to replace Jeff, and that means I get to go and do more of his work. On top of mine. Thankfully, my boss seems to get that and gave me a couple of hours off."

"I would love to get lunch with you, but I kind of used my lunch hour to work with a student."

Paris smiled, her expression turning warm. "That's wonderful. I mean, not the fact that you're not eating, but that you're such a great teacher. I don't know if I would have the patience."

"You learn it. Or...you just don't teach. At least, you shouldn't if that's not in your skill set." I shrugged. "But that doesn't matter. I love what I do, even though I'm tired right now, you know?"

"No, I don't. Because you didn't tell me about the rest of your date. I mean, you mentioned the whole accidental run-in thing, which, oh my God, how amazing is that? However, I don't really know much more."

"There really isn't much more to say outside of what I already told you."

After I had gotten home, Paris called again, this time on a four-way chat with the other girls so they could ask me exactly what had happened. Apparently, I had been a little too mysterious when I hung up with Paris during dinner. They had all been a mix of surprised, worried, and excited.

Considering that I was going through all of those same emotions, it was understandable.

"I think you already know everything," I said finally.

Paris raised a perfectly sculpted brow. "Really? So, there's been no contact since?"

"No," I said, my stomach clenching. And thank you for reminding me that he hasn't called or texted."

"First off, it's been less than forty-eight hours. And you have his number, as well. You could call him. After all, that is what this pact is about, right? Taking our futures into our own hands and forging our own paths. Along with friends."

I shook my head. "I was already on that path. It didn't work out. A literal organ was taken from someone's body."

"That *is* a problem. But that's not something we should focus on right now. Besides, it wouldn't have worked out between you and Stavros anyway."

"Why is that?"

Paris had the grace to wince. "Apparently, he is getting back together with his ex-wife. I didn't know they still had a connection outside of their daughter. I thought I knew everything. My research is clearly flawed. By the time we get to the next people on the list, including your next date—if this thing doesn't work out with Cross—then I will have my research down better."

I just shook my head, holding back a laugh. "I don't know. I feel like if I text or call him, it might ruin the bubble of what we shared. You know?"

"Maybe. Or perhaps you're missing an opportunity. I don't think you're ever going to know until you try," Paris said honestly.

She tucked her hair behind her ear before she added, "I'll let you be. But just know that part of the pact is possibly pushing you in the right direction. You took that oath, too, you need to be a part of it."

"There wasn't an oath." I paused. "Was there?"

Paris just smiled brightly.

"Pushing me in this direction might not be the best idea," I said honestly.

"Or maybe it will be the best one ever. Either way, don't give up hope. Maybe text him yourself."

I shook my head and said goodbye to Paris, not sure if I would reach out or not. I had more important things to worry about today.

It didn't matter that I kept thinking about Cross's smile or the way his hands had felt on mine.

I shook my head. *I have work to do.*

I finished up another set of office hours and then did some work on my research until it was time to head home. I had a slight headache, mostly because while I loved numbers, they sometimes didn't love me back. Plus, I had been stupid and hadn't worn my reading glasses until about an hour into my day.

I was still getting used to the fact that I had to wear

reading glasses, even though I wasn't reaching the age that my mother was when she got hers.

I frowned, wondering why I'd even thought about that. It'd been a while since I'd thought about my parents. The fact that Cross had asked about them during our date had surprised me, though it really shouldn't have. People always asked about families. They inquired about that, work, and friends. That was just how dating worked. Simply because I was out of practice didn't mean I didn't remember the rules.

I made it home, pulled into my garage, and shut the big slider before I even opened the car door. I had my pepper spray in my hand as I slid out of the vehicle and made my way to the entrance to the house.

I didn't even realize I was doing it most days. It was just something that I was used to now.

I couldn't help it. When you went through what I did, sometimes, the way you moved, even around your own home, meant that you didn't feel safe. Finding any way to create that feeling of safety was important.

I checked the security on the house and then made sure that everything was locked before setting down my bag and going to pour myself a glass of wine. It had been a long day, and I was tired.

Besides, a single glass of wine at night was good for your heart, right?

The studies on that changed daily, but I was going with it.

I had just taken my first sip when my phone buzzed. I frowned, looking at it.

It was probably one of the girls, wanting to know more about Cross or telling me exactly what was going to happen next with our plan.

I didn't know if I wanted to go through that anymore. It already hadn't turned out the way we expected, and I had a feeling that wasn't going to change anytime soon.

When I looked down at the cell, I saw that it wasn't one of the girls.

My heart sped up, and my hands dampened. Oh. *Oh.*

Cross: *Hey there. Sorry it took me a while to text you. I'm really not good at this. I overthought it the whole damn time.*

Cross: *I probably shouldn't have said that.*

Cross: *Or cursed.*

Cross: *Sorry.*

My shoulders sagged, and I grinned. Honestly, he couldn't have said anything better. He had said the perfect damn thing.

Because I wasn't good at this either.

Me: *I was thinking that I wasn't very good at this either. So, hi.*

That was good, right? I didn't want to overthink it. I tried my best to not overthink things during our one evening together. This would just have to be the same.

Cross: *I wasn't even sure you would want to hear from me. Then my sister said if I didn't text you, I would be an ass.*

Me: *You talked to your sister about us?*

Us? Great, maybe I should rethink what I was saying. There wasn't an us. And he had told his sister? What else had he said? Oh God, I didn't think I could go through with this.

Whatever *this* was.

Cross: *I tell her most things. Mostly because I need a sounding board, and she's good at keeping things to herself.*

Well...if he could be honest, so could I.

Me: *I'll be honest and say I told my friends, too.*

Cross: *I wouldn't have expected anything different. However, where does that put our date on your blind date plan?*

I laughed.

Me: *I think Paris has decided that this is going to be part of the plan. So, I'm sorry in advance if she somehow finds your contact information and forces you into another date with me.*

Cross: *Who said anything about forcing?*

Me: *Oh, really?*

Cross: *I am texting you, after all. I was going to call, but that seemed a bit too forward in this day of technology.*

I laughed again.

Me: *You're right. That is a bit forward.*

Cross: *Also, got to be up with what the kids are doing. Right? Anyway, here I am.*

Cross: *Texting. And I really fucking suck at it.*

Cross: *And hell, there I go, cursing again. Sorry.*

Me: *How fucking dare you?*

Cross: :)

I snorted.

Cross: *Anyway, I didn't know the rule of forty-eight hours or any other fucking shit that dating entails these days. And since we started on a different path than most people, I figured why not. So, hi.*

Me: *Hi.*

Cross: *Anyway, I'd love to take you out again.*

Tension slid through me, even as butterflies did a dance in my stomach.

Me: *I think that might be fun.*

Cross: *Really?*

Me: *Are you second-guessing already?*

Cross: *I told you I was terrible at this. I want to take you out. However, I'm a bit busy right now. I figured you* *must be too since this is the start of the semester, if I remember school right.*

Me: *You're right. And I have a couple of faculty meetings and dinners over the next week.*

Cross: *I guess that means we'll have to keep this evil texting thing up until we have time to plan something.*

Me: *That seems a bit scary.*

Cross: *Tell me about it.*

I smiled and texted a few more times about nothing, but the sensation of something new and unknown slid through me. Almost as if this were the beginning of something. I didn't want to think too hard about it or put too much into it, so I didn't. Instead, I smiled and slid my phone back into my bag after I said goodbye.

It wasn't a complete commitment, but it was a start.

He had texted, and he had more courage than I did, considering that I still wasn't sure if I would have texted him.

But he hadn't run screaming after our meeting. And that counted.

At least, I hoped it did.

My phone buzzed again, and I pulled it out, a smile on my face. I wondered what Cross wanted now.

When I looked down, the hairs on the back of my neck rose, and ice slid through my veins.

It was a text from an unknown number, completely

blocked, one that I wasn't going to be able to find on my own.

Unknown: *I see you.*

That was it, that was the text. Bile slid up my throat, and as I clutched the phone in my hands, I turned towards the counter and threw up the rest of my wine and the salad from earlier, right into the sink.

He couldn't see me. This couldn't be him. Only... maybe it was. Maybe he was here. He'd hit me before. He'd stalked me after. Had waited in my home when I was out and thought I was safe. He'd sent me letters during the trial. Had called and left messages telling me what he was going to do to me.

There were reasons I was so extreme in my home security. Why I was careful when I wasn't at home.

And, somehow, he was texting me.

How.

I wiped my face, turned on the water to clean up the mess, and then double-checked my locks.

I had my pepper spray in one hand, my phone in the other, and went to the corner where I could see all angles. And then I prayed even while calling the detective who'd handled my case. I needed to know if Thomas was still in California. If I was safe.

I needed to know it all, and yet I couldn't focus. I couldn't breathe.

All ideas of what I could have with Cross were gone from my mind.

I wasn't the person I had once been.

I couldn't believe in paths and hope anymore.

Because he was always watching.

Waiting.

I couldn't run from that.

Chapter 6

CROSS

I LOWERED MY HEAD AND FOCUSED ON THE WORK IN front of me, the bass from the speakers I had mounted to the wall thrumming in my ears. It let me concentrate, push out the rest of the world so I could work on what was in front of me, rather than what others needed from me.

I slid my fingers over the wood and then used my sander with the other hand, working on one of the arches for the bottom grooves. I was getting down to the nitty-gritty, the design parts that were beyond the engineering, beyond function, only for the aesthetics. The parts that called to the uniqueness, sometimes in subtle ways. That was the part I liked.

That was a lie.

I liked both parts. I loved every single aspect of my job, even the taxes and the paperwork and dealing with clients.

That was another lie, I didn't like the taxes, but I didn't mind doing them. Because that meant I had money in the bank and had to show the government that I was making something of myself.

I shook my head and went back to my project. I would probably have this part finished today, and after a few more days, I could get back to the final nit-picky parts, the polish. And then the clients could pick up the table and chairs.

It sounded like a lot of work, and probably more than some would want for a dining room set, but I'd fallen in love with woodworking when I was younger, and now it was a passion that had somehow become my career. The pieces I made weren't for everyone, and many of the crafts I worked on weren't high-end. The more highly detailed projects that took longer and went for a higher price supplemented some of my other smaller projects.

I hummed along to the music, getting into my work. Now, I could be an artist, a craftsman. That was something Arden would call me, not something I usually called myself. The more I thought about it, however, the more I didn't mind the term. I was getting better at realizing who I was, even if that idea seemed to change some days.

I got to a stopping point and went back over my work to see if there was anything I needed to touch up before I called it a night. I wanted to get back to my place since my brothers were heading over soon for beers and dinner. I didn't want to be the last one there, considering it was my house.

I'd invited Arden, but she had a girls' night scheduled with her sisters-in-law, so I let her be. I loved that she had another support system now, but I still wanted to be all big brother and wrap her in cotton wool.

It was hard not to be a little overbearing when her husband was out of town. All I wanted to do was make sure that she was doing well and continuously check up on her.

I put away my tools, cleaned up my station, turned off the music, and rolled my shoulders back as I headed out to the central area of the building. Chris was there, texting furiously. My guard instantly went up.

I didn't want to deal with him. I had been doing a decent job of ignoring him for the past couple of days, but that wasn't the best thing. After all, we still had to talk about exactly what we were doing with this business. And he had been avoiding me, just like I had been avoiding him.

Chris looked up from his phone before I had a chance to think about what I was going to say.

"Oh. Good. You're done. I was just heading out, and I wanted to see how you were doing."

"I was just on my way out, too. Is there something you wanted?" I asked. I wasn't in the mood to figure out what to do with Chris, and I actually had somewhere to be. Things had quieted down since I'd told him we needed to talk. I didn't think that everything would get better overnight, though. I really did need to either dissolve the partnership or find a better solution. Still, for now, he was acting as if everything was at least marginally on the level. And he wasn't annoying me that much.

The fact that that was my hard limit should worry me.

"Oh. Anything fun tonight?" he asked. I wasn't sure if he was actually interested.

When had we come to this? Chris used to be my friend. I had irrevocably tied my business and future to this man, and yet I didn't seem to know him anymore. Had I changed? Or had he?

Maybe it was the mixture of the two that had ruined it. "Just hanging out with my brothers."

Chris smiled, but it didn't reach his eyes. He didn't get along with my brothers. Mostly because Chris always tried to make sure they knew that he made good money. My brothers did well for themselves, too. But it was never good enough for Chris. Seriously, I needed to fix this. However, tonight wasn't the time to do it.

"Ah. Well then, have fun. I have a meeting with that client. You know? Cassidy?"

No, I didn't know her, but that was the point. Wasn't it? "Going to 59th?"

"Yes, that's the plan, at least at first. We'll see where it leads."

My brows rose. "She's your client. You'll see where *what* leads?"

He waved his hand at me. "You know I don't mix business with pleasure." He winked.

That was a lie.

"Anyway, I have things to do, and I'm sure you do, too. From the music, it sounded like you were really into it. Would you mind showing me what you're working on?"

"Maybe. I'm still at the stage where it's not ready for eyes." I had locked the door behind me, and he didn't have a key. Nor did I have a key to his studio. That's how it had always been. This was our art, and it was personal.

I didn't know exactly why I didn't want to show him. It just felt like something of mine, and I didn't want to share it.

Or maybe I was being paranoid.

Hell, that was just one more nail in the coffin, wasn't it?

"I see," Chris said, his voice smooth, if a little icy.

What did he see?

Chris continued. "I won't keep you, then. Have fun with your brothers. Wish me luck with this client."

"Is this the project you're hoping to make a lot of money on?"

"Oh, that's another one, but that's already on the line. Don't you worry, I'll be raking in the cash soon. You'll wish you had joined me."

"I'm doing just fine, Chris."

"And that's your problem, Cross. You're always just *fine*."

And on that note, Chris walked out, leaving me to close up the rest of the building. I didn't mind as it was something I did most days. But hell, he was really good at putting me in a shitty mood.

I got into my car and made it to my house, thankfully before my brothers got there, and quickly pulled out the lasagna I had made that morning. I shoved it into the oven, not bothering to preheat the damn thing, knowing that likely wasn't smart, but whatever. I really wasn't in the mood. And Arden was the better cook. I just followed her directions and used the sauce that she had put in my freezer.

The doorbell rang, and then Prior walked in, Macon and Nate with him.

I shook my head. "At least you rang the doorbell."

"You know us. We walk where we're not wanted," Macon said, a mock growl in his voice.

"Oh, shut up. You know you're wanted. I was just surprised that you rang the doorbell at all."

"We do have manners," Prior said, grinning. "And we brought beer and bread."

Nate moved to the kitchen island. "And I brought Italian salad fixings. You know, with the homemade dressing that Arden made for us that tastes just like the Olive Garden kind?"

"Hell yeah," I said, smirking. "You know, I'm sure Mom would want us to have wine with this, but I could really use a fucking beer."

"It was in the cooler in the car, so it's still cold," Macon said, uncapping one and handing it to me. We each took a beer, clinked bottles, and I chugged half of mine as the others stared at me after they'd taken their sips.

"You want to talk about it, big brother?" Prior asked.

"I fucking hate my job," I growled and then went to the oven to check on the lasagna.

"Chris is a douchebag. You need to dissolve the partnership. You don't need him."

I looked at Nate. "I might not need him for the clients I have, but a lot of our reputation is tied up in the two of us."

"I don't know if that's true," Macon said, frowning. "You guys have completely separate client lists at this point. Most of the time, you have to explain the *Chris* part of your Chris Cross company name," he added.

I shook my head. "I just don't know. I have a bad feeling."

"Come and help me with the salad, and then cut up some bread and finish your beer. Then, you can have another, and we can figure this out."

"You know, given all our jobs, I just wish one of us was a fucking lawyer," I grumbled.

Macon shrugged. "Sorry, big bro. We all decided to do our own things."

"Yes, I know, but I could really use some legal advice."

"I bet we know someone," Prior added.

"I thought once Liam got back from his tour, I'd talk to him."

"Or you can shoot him an email now," Nate said. "And not wait until he gets back. It's going to be what, a couple of weeks?"

"I know, but then I'll have to talk to Chris, and I don't want to," I grumbled.

"Very mature of you," Macon said. "Anyway, I still

have the name of the lawyer I used for my practice," he said.

"Maybe. Thanks. The guy I used retired," I said.

"They tend to do that once they reach seventy," Prior said. I rolled my eyes.

"Anyway, the lasagna will be a bit. I was late because I was into my work, then I got delayed even more with Chris."

"No worries," Nate said. "I could probably eat this entire salad on my own, though."

"That's why I brought a shit ton of bread," Prior said.

"I'm going to have to work out twice as hard tomorrow morning before my shift if I'm going to work this off," Macon said, tapping his flat abs.

"I'm sorry it's happening this way," Prior said, his voice soft as Macon and Nate began to set the table.

"Me, too," I said, sighing. "I honestly didn't know it was like this until I looked up at him one day and realized I hated him. Like, what the fuck?"

"He was always a bit egotistical, but who wasn't?" Prior said.

"I hope I wasn't that bad," I said wryly.

"No, you were too self-deprecating to be that bad," Nate said surprisingly.

"What do you mean?" I asked.

"It took Arden practically shoving your art in your

face for you to realize that you had talent," Nate explained.

"That's not true." At least, I didn't think it was.

"Totally true," Macon added.

"You've always put others before yourself, and thought that what you did on the side when you were in high school working at that carpenter shop to help pay for your car was just a fun little hobby. I know you went to school for business, thinking that you were going to open a shop with your art. But we all know that wasn't the case," Prior said.

I stood there, shocked. "What? Of course, I went in knowing what I wanted to do."

"No, you went in telling yourself that you were going to go for your dreams, but you always had a fallback plan of some form of business. Something that you could contribute to, but that wasn't about art on the surface. Because you were too damn scared," Nate said, and I frowned.

"Scared?"

Macon rolled his eyes. "See. You went too damn far with that. Now, he's going to be a growly asshole all night. Look at him with that big beard of his. Oh, like a big bear with a thorn in his paw."

I flipped them all off. "You know what? Fuck you. So I don't always believe in myself."

"But you believed in us," Prior said softly, and I looked up at him.

"You always did," Nate said. "And if Mom and Dad hadn't saved for college as they did, and if we hadn't gotten scholarships and gone to smaller state schools, you probably would have found a way to pay for all of us."

"I mean, we're still trying to find ways to shove money into Arden's hands, and she's married to a millionaire," Prior said sarcastically.

"She shouldn't have to rely on him," I said. "Plus, she makes good money herself. It's not my fault the American healthcare system is shitty to the point where she can't afford to do anything, even with fucking great insurance," I grumbled.

"You know, that soapbox was getting a little dusty," Prior said wryly.

"Oh, shut up. You know you're ranting right alongside me," I said.

"That is true. We all rant about it. However, back to the point," Macon added. "You look at who you are now, and at the art you create, and you believe in yourself. But you didn't let yourself put that foot forward until much later. And now, you're someone who sees what you're worth—at least what you think you're worth, even though I still feel like you're worth a bit more," Macon added with a shrug. "Anyway, you see that, but I don't think Chris sees the same. He's always wanted to be better. Or at least seen to be."

"And ensuring he was the one making lots of deals, getting the best clients, and making really fucking good money while making furniture? Nobody truly believes that happens anymore," Prior said.

"I know, we're a niche market, but millionaires and billionaires need fancy shit when they're not buying antiques," I said.

"And don't knock your clientele," Nate said. "They do pay your bills."

"They do, and I don't always work only for the millionaires and billionaires. Believe me. It's the custom pieces I like, and the ones I can donate to. But still, I guess you're right. I am doing marginally better than Chris these days."

"That you know. For all you know, you're doing a fuck ton better than he is, and he just keeps lying."

"I see the money he makes," I said.

"You see what he reports to the IRS," Macon said.

My heart raced. "I'll look into that. But, fuck. Our accountant is good, and even though I'm making more money than he is right now, it's got to be the truth. Steve wouldn't fuck around with my money."

"True, I just don't trust Chris."

"Was it always this way?" I asked.

"No," Prior said. "It's a new thing."

"Enough of this introspective shit," Nate said, grinning. "Now, Arden says you went on a date?" he asked, and the others looked at me.

"I'm going to box her ears," I grumbled.

"Hey, why didn't she tell me?" Macon asked.

"Or me? I'm her favorite twin." Nate leaned forward.

"You're her only twin," the three of us said, and then laughed.

"I see where I stand," Nate said.

"But, really, Arden told you?" I asked. "She's usually good at keeping secrets from us." Nate flinched, and I had to wonder what kind of secrets Nate had. But if he was keeping them from me, he probably had a reason.

"She sort of blurted it out," Prior said, blushing. "She was really apologetic, and I wasn't supposed to mention it, but then I felt bad about the secret. So, she didn't mean to say it, and she didn't tell me anything other than that you had a date. Then she slapped her hand over her mouth and kicked me out of the house."

I laughed, shaking my head. "That sounds like Arden. And since she already sounds like she's apologetic, I won't have to punish her."

"Good, because if you did, we'd have to beat you, and then it'd be a whole thing," Prior said.

"True.

"So?" Nate asked.

Macon raised a brow, silent as ever.

"It was a date. Her name was Hazel. She's nice." I didn't want to go into more detail since I was still figuring my shit out.

"And?" Prior pressed. "Are you going on another?"

"I don't know. Maybe. Just...we'll see."

I wasn't in the mood to get into too many details, and thankfully, they didn't ask for more. Mostly because the oven timer went off, and it was dinnertime.

They helped me move the lasagna out of the oven, and then we waited for it to cool while we chomped down on salad, and then ate some amazing pasta thanks to Arden's recipe. We also gorged ourselves with bread, and I finished my second beer while they were still on their firsts. The rest of them were driving, though the fact that they had all timed it so they would arrive at the same time just made me laugh.

We were our parents' children, always arriving five minutes before the allotted time, fifteen minutes if it wasn't family.

After dinner, they helped with the dishes, and then I walked them out, knowing we all had to work the next day. It was nice to have some family time, and considering that four of the five of us were single, it was easier than with most families. Arden's new family was all married now, or at least on the verge of getting married. Some of them were even having babies. That meant it was harder for Arden to get to dinners with all of them than it was for her to hang out with us. Maybe one day, when the rest of them finally settled down like our little sister had, getting together would be harder. But as it was, I liked the way things were. I liked being able to have time with my family, even if my parents had moved away.

I talked to them weekly, but it wasn't the same. Ever since they'd left, it'd just been the five of us kids, closer than ever.

I pulled out my phone and wondered if I should call them, and then thought of something different.

Something that probably wasn't the best idea, or maybe it was the perfect one.

Me: *Hey, are you awake?*

Hazel: *It's like 7:30. What time do you think I go to sleep?*

I grinned.

Me: *It's a school night. For all I know, this is your bedtime.*

Now I was thinking about her in bed, and I didn't like that my cock hardened. I didn't know her well enough to start fantasizing about her. At least that's what I told my dick.

Hazel: *I was just grading papers. You know us teachers, the red pen tells all.*

I winced.

Me: *That was like the worst part of doing homework, seeing what I fucked up on.*

Hazel: *You said you got your degree, so I guess you didn't fuck up that bad. Plus, there's a lot of math in your job. I'm sure you're pretty good at it.*

Me: *Just not calculus, which is fine, that can be all you.*

Hazel: *I'm glad you texted. Kind of.*

From what I knew about her, I knew that had to be hard, opening herself up even just a little. So I did the same. After all, we were both trying to figure out precisely what this was, accidental date or not.

Me: *I'm glad I texted as well.*

I let out a breath.

Me: *So, can I take you out this weekend?*

There was a long enough pause that I thought maybe I'd fucked up. Was I moving too fast? Or did she just want to be friends? Hell, I really wasn't good at this.

Hazel: *Maybe. I have a lot of things to think about, though.*

I had no idea what to do about that cryptic comment. Before I could say anything else, she texted again.

Hazel: *I have to get back to grading, but thanks for texting. Good to know you're not an asshole.*

I frowned and texted back.

Me: *Good to know. Sleep tight, Hazel.*

Hazel: *You too.*

Then that was it, no more dots telling me she was texting again.

Had I spooked her?

Hell, I didn't know, but something was off. Things seemed to be going right, and then she backed away.

Maybe it wasn't about me, or perhaps the whole idea of what we could have had was just that, an idea.

I didn't know, but that cryptic text on top of everything that was going on with Chris told me that maybe I should go to bed early like I had said she might be doing. Because I had no idea what the fuck I was going to do, and now I was more confused than ever.

Chapter 7

HAZEL

I RAN, MY FEET SLAMMING INTO THE GROUND, slapping against the pavement since I was barefoot, rain coating my hair, my shoulders, forcing my silk dress to cling to me.

I didn't know why I was barefoot, nor why I was wearing a dress, but I ran.

I ran.

My heart thundered in my ears, and bile filled my throat. It was so real, I could taste it. Everything was just so real.

The terror in my heart, the fact that I could barely catch

my breath, all of it told me that this wasn't a joke, it wasn't a dream. This was real. I couldn't focus, couldn't breathe.

A dark laugh slid along my skin, deep as if it were from hell itself. I screamed, but no sound came out. There was nowhere for me to go, no one for me to run to. No one could hear me scream, just like in the horror movies that I refused to watch anymore.

I found myself in a forest, lightning flashing brightly amongst the leaves as I ran, twigs digging into my feet, leaving a trail of blood. A branch slapped me in the face, a thin one so it only left a bloody line down my flesh, but I kept running. Mud slid between my toes, and I slipped, slid. But I kept going. I had to.

The laugh was closer now, and I could feel his breath on my neck.

I kept running, kept fighting, and I found myself in front of a house, one that was so familiar.

I slammed my fist against the door, screaming. "Let me in! Help! Please, help me!"

The doorknob twisted, and light blinded me, but I could see the shadow within, and I knew it wasn't the man who laughed. No, it was something far scarier.

I looked at a face that was my own, the visage of the unknowing, someone who had thought they knew everything.

I looked back at myself in my cardigan and soft cashmere pants. And I saw the bruise on my cheek, the innocence gone from my gaze.

I saw myself, the person I had once been, the moment everything had changed.

And then the laugh came again, and we both screamed.

I woke up, my body shaking, but I was fine.

I was alive.

I was whole.

And I was safe.

I ran my hands over my body, checking to make sure nothing was wrong. I noticed that I was sweat-slick, but that was fine. I was always covered in sweat when I woke up from those dreams.

Of course, the twisted ending of that particular dream had been new, as I had mixed two night terrors that I normally had. However, I wasn't too surprised by that. After all, knowing that he was out of jail meant that these dreams would keep coming, even if he wasn't anywhere near me.

It had just been a text, a taunt, but he wouldn't come near me.

He knew that if he tried, he would end up in jail for longer than the four years he'd already spent there.

That would be the third strike, and there was no coming back from that.

And if I kept telling myself that, that I would be safe because of the legal system, maybe I would one day believe it.

Thomas was not going to hurt me. I wouldn't let him.

I slid out of bed, my pepper spray in one hand, my phone in the other, and walked around the house in my panties and a tank top, ensuring that all the windows were locked, all the blinds were shut tight, and my doors had all of their locks engaged. I went through my video surveillance system, ensuring that nobody had come around creeping when I was asleep. I found nothing.

I was as safe as I was going to get—except for when I slept.

At those times, I couldn't force the dreams away.

It was hard enough when I was awake. When I was awake, I couldn't hold back the thoughts. I could, just not well enough. When I dreamt, they never went away. When I wasn't asleep, I could tell myself that everything was fine, and the safety I had given myself was enough.

I wasn't sure if that fear would ever go away entirely, and now that Thomas was out of jail, there would never be true safety. Especially not when he had already sent a text trying to threaten me.

I didn't know if he was near, or if he was watching. But it didn't matter. I had to get over it.

I had to believe.

Because I had things to do.

I showered, scrubbing my skin longer than usual because I wanted the remembered feel of his breath on the back of my neck to go away.

I didn't think it would ever actually go away.

After, I stood there in a towel, blew out my hair, and put on the beginnings of my makeup.

I had things to do for the day, papers to grade, research to go over. Later tonight, if I actually let myself, I had a date.

Not my first one since Thomas, and not even my first date with Cross, but it was still like it was the first for everything. Perhaps because it was something deliberate this time? I had agreed to this second date. It wasn't the first that had been accidental.

I didn't know what it was, but it worried me enough that I couldn't focus. I was so scared.

What if Thomas was watching? What if he ignored the restraining order? After all, it was merely a piece of paper.

And that couldn't protect me.

I put on comfortable clothing, knowing I would change later, and then went to my office to begin work.

An hour in, and two cups of coffee later, my phone rang, and I jumped.

I cursed myself, the fear flooding my body and running down to my fingers as I calmed my breathing.

It wasn't Thomas. No, he wouldn't call. He would lurk, he would text, and he would save his voice and his laughter and his breath for the last.

Bile filled my throat again, tasting just like it had in my dream. I answered the phone.

"Hello?" I asked, my voice shaky.

"What's wrong?" Paris asked.

"Just lost in grading, I suppose," I lied.

"Talk to me, what's wrong?" Paris asked again.

My friend was like a dog with a bone and wouldn't let me be until she figured out what was wrong. While I loved that about her sometimes, right now, I was just tired.

Maybe tonight wouldn't be the best night to go out on a date with Cross. I clearly wasn't ready, and I would only make things worse by pretending that I was.

"I'm really doing fine," I said, my voice stronger this time. "Just a little lost in grading."

"That's a lie, and we both know it, but I'll let you keep to that if you want. Just know that I'm here for you. And so are the others. Talk to them if I'm too much for you."

I winced, even though she couldn't see me. "It's not you. I promise. I just need to think. I love you, and I trust you with so much. You're never too much for me," I said honestly. Paris might be a lot to handle for some, but I loved that about her. She never took no for an answer, and she was so strong. I was a little envious.

I also knew that Paris had her own issues when it came to that strength. It was a shield, and not everybody understood that. They didn't need to. Because it was for her and her alone. And she had her reasons.

"If you're sure," Paris said. "Anyway, I just wanted to check in with you to see if you're ready for tonight."

I groaned. "I still don't know why I said yes," I said truthfully.

"Because you want to go on a date with him for real?" she asked, and I snorted. It was good to laugh, mostly because I didn't know why I was doing it.

"Do you want us to come over and have some girls' time to help you pick out what to wear and do your hair?" Paris asked. This time, I laughed in truth.

"I'm really all right. I have done this before, you know."

"Yes, you've done this before. But this is a little different, isn't it?" she asked.

"I don't want it to be too different," I said honestly. "It's been a while since I've been on a second date."

"If it helps, you can think of it as a second first date since the first one was out of the box," she said.

"Maybe. Or perhaps I'm just going to lose my mind. We're going out to dinner, and we're meeting there. Mostly because I don't want him to know where I live," I said quickly and then regretted it instantly.

There was a pause, and I knew that Paris was trying to think of the best thing to say. "I don't blame you. All women need to feel safe. And with what you've been through? You need to be extra careful. It's understandable that you wouldn't want people to know where you live, especially when you don't know him. I have friends, someone who can run a background check on him if you want," Paris said quickly. "I mean, we've already done the whole social media thing, but I'm sure there are other people we can ask."

I shook my head and then remembered that she couldn't actually see me.

"I don't need you to run a background check." I had already done that, but I didn't tell her as much. After all, some people from my past had tried to help me with Thomas. They hadn't failed, precisely, but nobody had won with the final outcome.

"Anyway, all of us will come over and help you get ready if you want," Paris said again.

"I'm just going to finish grading, get through some of my other work for the day, and then I'll get ready."

"Wow, that sounds so romantic for how you're going

to get ready for this big date," Paris said, pure sarcasm in her tone.

"Oh, shush. I have things to do, and I can't focus my entire life on prepping for a date that'll probably just end up a disaster."

I hadn't meant to say that last part.

"So, you're going into it thinking it'll be a pure disaster?" Paris asked.

"No, I'm going into it without hope for the best. If I do that, I'll be safer."

"That's a telling statement," Paris said dryly. "Just remember, we went into this whole pact of ours to try and branch out. Not to be alone anymore. If you go into your date thinking that it's going to end badly, then you're going to create a self-fulfilling prophecy."

"Or, maybe that's just how life is." I paused. "I'm not good at this, Paris. I shouldn't have been the first one. Myra would've been better at this. Or even you."

Paris laughed. "I'm not going to take that as a jab with you adding the *even*. And maybe the others will be better than us at dating. But if that was the case thus far, we wouldn't be here at all."

"I just don't want to end up ruining things any more than they already are," I said honestly.

"But what do you mean by that?" Paris asked.

I frowned. "I have no idea. I just know I wasn't happy

before. And Cross seems like a great guy. He was great because it was fun and unexpected. When I see him again, what if it's anything but?"

"You won't know until you try," Paris said.

"You know, I'm going to be just as pushy as you are when you do this."

"Perhaps. But first, you have to get through your sets of dates."

"Wait, I think we mixed a big loophole in this whole dating pact thing," I said suddenly, leaning forward. "When does the next person start?"

"When we are all satisfied that you have fulfilled your promise."

"What does that mean? And don't you dare say marriage. Because that's ridiculous."

"You're the one who brought it up. And we're not exactly clear on all the rules," Paris admitted.

"Oh, great. What's going to happen is, I'm going to be the only one who has to do any of this, and you guys are just going to go off with your perfect little lives and never have to deal with the embarrassment of sitting down with a guy who isn't your actual date."

"No, we are all going to go on dates with random people that will probably turn out worse. After all, you met a wonderful man, at least as much as you know so far, and you're going on a second date with him tonight. Enjoy yourself, and don't worry. When the time is right, the next person will have their time."

"You're the next person, Paris." I paused. "In fact, I'm going to talk with Dakota and Myra. We need to start working on you."

"Let's not rush things," Paris said quickly, and I laughed.

"See? You don't like it when the shoe is on the other foot."

"I love all shoes, don't worry. When my time comes, whenever that may be, I will give in."

I laughed for real this time, a deep belly laugh that I knew Paris was likely grimacing at, even if I couldn't see her face.

"Have fun tonight," Paris said. "Seriously. Just remember that you're allowed to have fun."

"I'll try," I said, and then we hung up, and I looked down at my grading. I knew I wasn't going to finish today.

No, I was going to get ready for my date and wonder exactly how this had happened.

I went to my bedroom and opened my closet, wondering how I had gotten ready the first time. I hadn't had this nervousness wrapping around me like it was now. Perhaps because whatever would have happened with Stavros would have been mere fantasy.

A pact made between friends that didn't seem quite real.

I had gone through the motions, not knowing exactly how I should feel. I'd put on a sexy but not too revealing dress, did my hair and makeup like I'd been taught—an armor and a weapon in the hands of masters, as my mother had once said—and had gone to a swanky bar in Boulder—the swankiest. I had gone, knowing full well that I would never see that man again. Because he hadn't been real.

And because I'd never met him—still hadn't—he wouldn't ever be real to me. While I wished him the best of luck with his ex-wife and hoped his child had all the happiness in the world, he would never be real to me.

And for someone who went through dreams in life like I had, who craved concrete math and proof, reality was what I needed to breathe, to live, to *survive*.

Tonight wouldn't be like before. It would be different.

I knew Cross—at least as much as I could know a man I had accidentally gone on a date with.

I had spoken to him, had touched him—in the most chaste of ways, of course—and I knew he was real.

As I chose my outfit with care, making precise decisions since it was the only way I would be able to focus tonight, I wondered yet again how I had ended up here.

When I found myself looking in the mirror, my eyes

wide, my face pale with a touch of color on my cheeks, I knew I couldn't back down now.

Even as I did my best to ignore the memory of hot breath on my neck from a dream that wasn't merely a dream, I knew I had to take these next steps.

I didn't want to be a person who hid in fear any longer.

The only problem was, I didn't know what kind of person I wanted—*needed*—to be.

And the answer to that wasn't something I could get from dreams or math or even dates with a man who made me smile.

That would come from somewhere far different.

From me.

Chapter 8

CROSS

"I DIDN'T THINK I WOULD NEED HELP GETTING READY for tonight," I said as I opened the door to my entire family.

Macon, Prior, Nate, Arden, and even Liam walked through, their hands thankfully empty, though all looked at me.

"Seriously, what are you doing here?"

"You're going on a date," Arden said, going up on her tiptoes to kiss my cheek. I reached around and gave her a hug, nodding at the guys.

"I know I'm going on a date. I still don't know why

you think I need your help, though. I've been dating for quite a while."

"Actually, it's been a while from what I hear," Liam said, running his tongue over his teeth.

I flipped off my brother-in-law. Liam just winked, a grin on his face.

"Be nice. That is the future father of my children right there," Arden said.

My eyes widened. I hadn't heard my sister talk about children in a while. It was kind of nice.

"Really? That's what you're going with?" I said, keeping my voice light. I knew Arden wasn't going to be able to carry a child, something she had mentioned a few times since she had been diagnosed. It wasn't just the lupus that had led to that conclusion, but a few other things, as well. We had all been very careful not to bother her with any questions about that, at least until she was ready.

"That was my awkward way of saying that Liam and I are going to try adopting," she said, clapping her hands in front of herself. She blushed, her eyes filling with tears as she leaned into her husband. I looked at my brothers, and then all of us grinned widely, opening our arms. A huge Brady brother and sister and Liam group hug commenced.

"Really? You know I think that is fucking amazing

news," I said.

"Seriously? I can't wait to be an uncle," Prior said, rubbing his hands together. "I mean, think about all the shit I could teach that kid."

"You are not letting my child become a troublemaker," Arden said, and Liam just raised a brow.

"Between my family and yours, I'm pretty sure the wide array of uncles and aunts involved is going to let that kid get away with anything they want. At least until they reach an age where they can't get away with anything," Liam said honestly, and I laughed.

"That sounds about right. We'll spoil your kid no matter what, but when they become a teenager, we will make sure they don't get into trouble. I mean, that is the uncle and aunt way," I said.

"Anything you need from us, we're here," Macon said, and we all nodded solemnly.

"My twin is having a baby. This is going to be so exciting." Nate folded his arms over his chest and grinned.

Arden rolled her eyes. "We literally just decided, and I was going to wait to tell you. It kind of just slipped out."

"You know we're going to have to tell my family. Because if my sister hears that your brothers heard before her, she's going to launch a reign of terror."

I leaned forward. "She's married now. She's calmer."

We all paused and then broke out into laughter.

"So she might not be calm. But seriously, I love your sister, and she's going to be a fantastic aunt. Just know that it's going to take a while for everything to happen. I mean, it could be years. Are you trying for a baby? Or any age in particular?" I asked.

"Any age," Arden said, squeezing her husband's hand tightly. "We just want a child who needs a home and us. We know it's not going to be easy, but seriously, we all know that living and raising children isn't easy no matter what."

"Well," I said, letting out a breath.

"You're right about that, but hell, I'm so excited for you," I said, smiling.

"I'm excited for us, too." She shook her head and then bounced on her feet. "However, this was totally not supposed to be about us."

"You're always welcome to have it be about you, babe," Liam said, kissing the top of her head.

"So, if you aren't here to tell me that news, why are you here?" I asked again, suddenly a little nervous.

"You're going on your second date with this woman. We want to make sure you don't fuck it up," Prior said, grinning.

I narrowed my eyes. "Why do you think I'm going to fuck it up?"

"Because you're stressed out about work and probably

about us because you're always messed up over family, and you're going to be more focused on that than making sure you treat her like you could have a future together," Nate said.

We all looked at Nate, blinking.

"I can't believe you just said that. You're not always so insightful."

Nate flipped us off.

"I am the most insightful brother. It's the twin thing," he said, looking at Arden.

She shrugged. "He's right."

"Hey," Macon and I said together. And then we looked at Prior, who hadn't complained.

Our other brother just shrugged. "I'm the funny one, Macon is the quiet, growly one, Cross is the loud, growly one, and I guess that makes Nate the sensitive one. Although I suppose, sometimes, that could be Macon. I don't know, there are a lot of us. It gets confusing at times."

I rolled my eyes. "Seriously, though, why are you here?"

"The honest answer is that we were on our way out to dinner, and we figured we would stop by and annoy you," Liam said, and I laughed.

"That is an honest answer. I appreciate it. Thank you."

"No problem. However, just remember that all of my siblings were up in my business the entire time I was seeing Arden, and are pretty much going to be that way for the rest of our lives. It's going to be an issue forever, but I like it. You're the eldest, like I am. You're going to have to get over it. While you'll likely want to growl and take care of everyone else, they're going to want to do the same for you. It's payback."

"Now, who's the insightful one?" Nate said, and I shook my head.

"You guys go get food. Do your thing. I'm off to meet Hazel."

Nerves made my belly clench, but I ignored them. Just because this was our first date—well, our first *real* date rather than an accidental one—didn't make it any different. It was just that I didn't have time to get nervous before. It had been a while since I had been on a date, and I wasn't sure I was any good at it.

The fact that I wasn't sure she even wanted to go on a date with me, that she hadn't simply been talked into it, worried me too.

But it was fine. I just had to keep from thinking so hard.

"So, do you need help getting ready?" Nate asked, his gaze searching mine.

"What do you mean by that?" I asked.

"Um?" Arden began. "How do I say this delicately?" I looked at her, putting on my best innocent and confused face.

"What? I don't look ready for my date?" I looked down at my track shorts, flip-flop slides, white socks— because my feet were cold, and I apparently wanted to look like a fashion faux pas that made even my teeth ache —and shirt with bleach on it.

"I don't look ready?"

"Please tell me you're joking," Prior implored.

"He's joking," Macon said, deadpan. "You're not that much of a fucking idiot."

"Of course, I'm not," I said. "For the love of God, I might be out of practice with dating, but I'm not that bad," I said honestly.

The others looked at me, and I threw my hands up into the air.

"You're wearing sandals with socks," Arden said. "How am I supposed to keep from questioning your motives? What's the plan here? Seriously, you are wearing sandals with socks."

"My feet were cold," I said.

"Then put on fucking slippers," Prior said.

"The slippers were in the other room. My socks were nearer. The sandals were close. I didn't feel like going upstairs."

"Laziness is no excuse for wearing socks with sandals," Nate said, laughing.

"I'm not going to wear socks and sandals ever again. I promise." I threw my hands up again, but nobody looked like they believed me.

Honestly, I didn't know if I believed myself. It was a horrible fashion choice, but I was comfy. And, apparently, now an old man. Because that is who wore socks and sandals. Old men. At least, according to the looks on my family member's faces.

"You're not really going to help me pick out something to wear, are you?"

"Don't tempt me," Arden said, tapping her foot. "I don't know. It could be good practice for when I'm helping my children."

"You know, that is a good idea," Liam said, and I rubbed my temples. "I swear I'm not going to wear this."

"And you promise never to wear socks and sandals again?" Macon asked, seriousness in his tone.

"I promise." I threw my hands up into the air for a third time. "Go, eat. Let me live my life in peace."

Prior shook his head. "As long as you're not living your life in your current outfit, that is fine. Just don't go out in public. You have the Brady name attached to you. Don't tarnish it."

"Considering that our name is tied to a very famously

dorky yet amazing family, I'm pretty sure I'm not going to be the one that does that," I said honestly.

"Go get changed. I promise we won't be here when you get back. But, have fun, be good, and don't fuck it up," Arden said, a wide smile on her face.

"I love it when you curse," Liam said. "Makes me feel a little bit better about all the words that come out of my mouth."

"When we have that child in our home, we're going to have to stop cursing." All of us looked at each other and then at Liam.

"Between the Montgomerys and the Bradys, that is going to be difficult."

"We'll figure it out," I said and then held my baby sister close. I kissed her on the top of the head and let out a deep breath. "I'm happy for you, baby sis."

"And I'm happy for you. Now, have fun. Don't think too hard, and just be yourself. She'll love you, just like we do."

"I hope we don't love him like we hope she will," Prior said. "Because you know that's against the law and shit. And I know the other more famous Bradys might joke around like that's cool and all, but that's not us," Prior said and then ducked as Macon slapped the back of his head.

"Hey, watch the hair."

"Maybe stop making incest jokes? I don't know,"

Macon said, and then he lifted his chin at me. Suddenly, they were gone, leaving me standing there, wondering how the hell I was going to get serious with a woman when they had to deal with my family. I loved them all, but they were a little much. And then I remembered how overprotective and growly I had been when Arden was first dating Liam, and realized that I was part of the problem.

I went up to my bedroom and quickly changed, wearing decent slip-on leather shoes rather than socks with sandals, a mistake I wouldn't make again anytime soon. Then, I headed to the restaurant. We were going to an Asian fusion place that had excellent sushi, and their version of fusion meant there was some fantastic Japanese food on the menu as well as some Korean barbecue. My stomach grumbled just thinking about it.

Hazel had nixed the idea of me picking her up, and while I understood that, she had said it so quickly and force-fully that I was afraid I had heard some fear in her voice. I might've just been projecting, though. I wasn't sure. She was likely hiding a few things, considering we had only met in person once. And I understood that she didn't need to tell me everything. But I did have to wonder why she'd sounded so scared, and a little reluctant to go on a date with me at all.

Again, maybe I was just projecting.

I pulled into the parking lot, then, as I approached the building, I opened the door right as someone walked near me. I turned and smiled.

Hazel wore form-fitting black jeans that had a little sparkle to them, a flowy black top that showcased her boobs but flared out at her hips, black boots with stiletto heels, and a leather jacket with rhinestones on the collar. It was a mix of sparkle and punk and sophistication all in one, paired with her black clutch that I had a feeling looked like Chanel, though I couldn't see the brand too well.

"I guess I'm right on time," I said, then leaned down to brush her hair off her shoulder. Her eyes widened for a fraction of a second, but she didn't move away. I didn't lean down to hug her or to touch her any more than I had. I didn't kiss her. I didn't do anything like that. I didn't want to worry her more than I thought maybe she already was.

After all, she looked a little bit like a deer caught in headlights.

Or, like usual lately, perhaps I was just projecting.

"That was good timing. You know, because being on time is nearly being late," she said and then grinned.

"I feel the same way. Sometimes, I get someplace so early, that if I don't feel comfortable enough sitting at the bar and getting something to drink while waiting, I'll just sit in my car and wait."

"I had to hold myself back from being early enough to sit in my car," she said honestly, and I shook my head, grinning.

"After you," I said, leading her toward the hostess stand. "I already think that this date thing is working out pretty well."

She smiled at me, and I could have slapped myself. I really wasn't good at this whole dating thing. For being so good with human interaction most of the time, I couldn't figure this out. Maybe it was just with her? Perhaps because she made me feel awkward, not that I knew why.

"Hi, party of two?" the hostess asked, her gaze on mine. She didn't even look at Hazel, and I frowned. I reached around and put my hand on the small of Hazel's back, and she didn't startle. Instead, she sank into my touch, and I held back a satisfied smile. The hostess noticed the movement as I'd intended, but she didn't seem to care. Instead, she raked me with that hungry gaze of hers, and I nodded.

"Yes, for two."

"Right this way," she said and turned on her heels before sashaying towards the table.

I did my best not to let my gaze move down to her ass, considering that it swayed back and forth. Seriously?

What would this woman think if she had seen me with socks and sandals? For some reason, I had a feeling that while Hazel would look shocked for a minute, and probably make fun of me, she wouldn't run away screaming like I thought maybe this woman would.

Or maybe I was just thinking a little too hard about that.

We took our seats, and I raised a brow when the hostess handed me both menus before walking away, her hips rolling all the while.

"It's good to know I exist," Hazel said and then snorted. I handed her a menu, shaking my head.

"I've never actually had someone be that obvious before."

"Really? You see yourself in the mirror. You're not ugly. And you have that whole...thing about you." She waved her hand in front of me, and I grinned.

"Thing?"

"Oh, shush. You know that you're handsome, and you have that smile. And you just seem like a nice guy. Maybe a little dangerous with that beard and ink, but these days, that's almost the norm."

"Thanks," I said dryly.

She winced. "Sorry. I didn't mean anything by that. I'm just saying that there's that whole meme going around, you know, where tattooed men used to mean bikers and murderers, and now, it's baristas that like a nice Bearnaise sauce or something like that."

"I think it was a balsamic reduction," I said, and we both laughed.

"Sorry, all I'm saying is that I don't really like being ignored like that. Not that I like the attention focused on me completely, I get enough of that while teaching, but that was kind of rude."

"I could say something," I said honestly.

"Please don't. Complaining that a hot woman finds *you* hot is a little much."

"Then I will be honest and say that I didn't really notice if she was hot or not," I said.

She snorted again. "Really?"

"No, and this is going to sound like a line, but it's not. I was too busy thinking about you. And this is why I'm not good at this whole dating thing, I say the cheesiest shit."

But she grinned, her eyes warm and clear.

"It might've been really cheesy, but thank you for that. Now, I'm starving, so if I happen to eat like two meals of food, just pretend that I'm dainty and sweet."

"I'm starving, too. I kind of skipped most of my meals today, trying to get some work done." My stomach took that moment to growl, loud enough for both of us to notice, and she grinned.

"What if we order a few things to share? I don't know if I'm going about this dating thing correctly by not eating a small salad and pretending that I'm not going to want to steal what's left on your plate, but I've been nervous all day. And I'm going to be honest about that. So, I didn't eat."

"I've been a little nervous, too. I think it's because of the whole non-accidental thing."

"Right? Who would've thought that this would feel more nerve-wracking than the blind date to begin with?"

"Maybe it's because we've actually met each other, and now we have to see if what we remember is something that we like."

"You're really not as bad at this as you think you are," she said softly. I swallowed hard. This was getting interesting.

"How about we order a big plate of sushi, as much as we can handle, a couple of soups, maybe a thing of spring rolls, and then a bulgogi and a yakisoba. We can share as much as we're able, and then split the takeout."

"Sold. But we have to eat all the sushi here because leftover sushi is gross and probably a health hazard."

I grinned. "That sounds amazing."

As the waiter goggled when we ordered everything, I laughed and leaned in, wanting to know more about Hazel.

Because I liked this woman. I liked the way she made me smile.

And while I knew I had other things to worry about, things that were important, I wanted to know what made her tick. I wanted to know her.

I wanted to know exactly why she hadn't been on a date before that blind date of hers that I'd crashed.

But right then, we were too busy smiling and gorging ourselves on sushi, so I didn't ask.

But I did lean in, because I wanted to know more. I wanted to know her.

This wasn't a blind date, and it wasn't an accidental one either. And I already knew I didn't want it to be the last one.

That surprised me more than anything.

By the end of the date, I had to hold my breath. Not only because of the temptation in front of me, but because of the sheer amount of food we'd eaten.

I leaned against the light pole near Hazel's car, one hand full of leftovers, the other on my stomach. "I think I ate too much."

Hazel leaned against her car, her pose mimicking mine. "I *know* I did." She grinned. "I know I'm supposed to be all cute and sexy or whatever for a date, but diving headfirst into bulgogi and sushi was so much better than trying to be something I wasn't just then."

I straightened, my gut tightening even though I was full. "You're still sexy, Hazel. It's in the way you laugh, the way your eyes brighten when you talk about your work. The fact that you *did* dive headfirst, right alongside me. I would have asked you out again because of the way you made me laugh, but you should know that I'll beg if I have to on top of that because you're damn sexy."

I probably shouldn't have said that, but there was no taking it back now.

She blinked wide eyes at me, her mouth parting. "Oh."

"Oh." I moved closer. She didn't flinch, but she *did* stiffen. "Can I kiss you?"

"You're asking?" Surprise was evident in her tone.

"Always. I'll never kiss you, touch you, or do *anything* without asking you first." I didn't know the whole story, but the way she moved around strangers, including me, told me that I needed to tread carefully. "Just a kiss. Nothing more." *Tonight.*

"Okay." She paused. "A kiss." She paused again. "Not that I might not want more in the future, but for now, let's go slow." She said the last part so quickly and blushed so red that I couldn't help but smile.

"I can do that." And then I leaned in, my lips so close to hers I could feel the heat of her. And then I waited.

She moved forward a fraction of an inch, and I let

myself go. I swallowed up the distance between us. Her lips were soft, her mouth parted, and I leaned in a bit, wanting more, but knowing this wasn't the place for that.

It wasn't long enough, a bare moment of tranquility and heat and need, but when I moved back, her eyes were wide, just like mine, and then she smiled. A small one, but an expression I knew I'd never forget.

"Well, then," I whispered, then cleared my throat. "I'm glad we finally did that."

"After two dates?" She swallowed hard. "Yes, I'm glad we did, as well."

So proper.

I fucking *loved* it.

"Again?" I asked, then shook my head when her gaze moved to my lips. My cock twitched, but I refrained from moving any more than I had. We were in public after all, standing under a bright lamp where anyone could see.

Possibly the safest place to park...though I didn't know why I'd thought that just then.

"Go out with me again."

"When?" she asked, then smiled. "I mean...sure. Yes. I'd like to."

"And not only for your pact?" I asked, unsure why I'd said that.

She smiled widely. "No, though the girls will be happy to hear that. Maybe it means it's Paris's turn."

I smiled at that. "That sounds like a plan." I helped her into her car and brushed my fingers along her collarbone, loving the way she pinked at the contact. "Text me when you get home?"

She frowned.

"I just want to know that you're safe."

"I...I can do that." She paused again. "I...I like that you care."

That was an odd thing to say, but hell, she should probably get used to my overprotectiveness. "Good. Because I should warn you, I'm a bear when it comes to making sure those I care about are safe."

"And do you care about me, Cross Brady?" she asked, something odd in her tone.

I leaned forward, my gaze on hers. "Yes, Hazel. I do. And I suppose that's something new *both* of us will have to learn how to navigate."

She smiled again, and I wondered what that meant, but I didn't ask. Instead, I closed her door, then watched her drive away, leaving me standing there with leftover Korean food, a hard-on, and confusion written over every inch of my face...and my heart.

Chapter 9

H AZEL

I STOOD AT THE FRONT DOOR, MY HEART RACING, BUT not out of fear. Mostly anxiety. Though considering that I felt like anxiety wearing a cardigan most days, this shouldn't be any different. I just really didn't want to ring the doorbell or knock. I did not want to go inside.

And then a voice came from the intercom on the doorbell. The fact that I had forgotten she had a video doorbell, told me my anxiety had reached a new level.

"Are you just going to stand here on Dakota's porch for the rest of the day? You should just come in. We unlocked the door for you."

I crossed my eyes at Paris's tone. "It's not safe to leave your door unlocked," I said, a little fear in my voice.

"We unlocked it when we saw you coming up. However, we will come out there if we have to."

The door opened on Paris's words, and I looked at Dakota, who just shook her head, a smile playing on her face.

"Paris and Joshua stole my phone, so I apologize for the way she answered." Dakota opened her arms, and I went into the offered hug, leaning in to the woman's hold. Dakota was quieter than the rest of us, probably because she had a six-year-old boy living with her, and because she was continually having to deal with noise—as well as being a mom. Since Paris was the loudest of us, it only meant that Dakota could finally rest. Or maybe I was thinking too hard.

"Thanks for having me over for brunch," I said, actually meaning it. I might be having a nervous breakdown for a variety of reasons, but I needed my girls. And brunch. "My hands were full, by the way, so I wouldn't have been able to turn the doorknob easily," I said honestly, and Dakota grinned, looking down at the plate in my hands.

"Oh, you made your little apple tartlette thingies," she said, taking the tray from me. "I love these so much."

"I was trading them for your goodies, and they aren't that hard to make because I cheated this time."

I winced, and Dakota just laughed. "I'm a mom, I often cheat when it comes to saving time while making dinner or any type of food," she said. "Store-bought pastry? It still looks amazing."

"Yes, but now I feel bad." Dakota always made hers from scratch.

"You were not going to make puff pastry from scratch for us," Myra said. "Not during this part of the semester anyway. And I hear you were out late with a certain sexy, bearded man," Myra said, leaning forward to kiss me on the cheek. It was an air kiss, the type we had done forever, and we both froze before laughing. It was part of our old lives, the ones where we did brunch and champagne and pretended that we liked the rest of the people we were with. She shook her head and then hugged me tightly. I hugged her back, not caring that if we had been wearing silk or pressed linen like the old days, it would have left wrinkles. Or God forbid, actually embraced each other in public like we liked one another.

"I love when you guys are all awkward about the fact that you knew each other when you were old money," Paris said, drawing out the words so it sounded like she was a fake British person.

"Sometimes those things are just ingrained in you. I

found myself drinking a mug of coffee with my pinky out the other day. A mug," Myra said, and I laughed.

"I know, how shocking. But we'll do better."

"Exactly. I will get you to drink beer out of the bottle one day," Dakota said, shaking her head as Joshua came running up, his hands in the air.

"Aunt Hazel! You're here!"

Joshua was six, and at the point where he only spoke in exclamation points. He did not calm down unless he was doing homework, and then he grumbled. However, he was just starting some math classes, and that was my favorite part. Dakota could teach him on her own, considering she was brilliant, owned her own business, and used to do all of her own accounting until recently. However, she let me pretend that I was truly needed for Joshua, and I sometimes got to help him with his schoolwork.

She was the only one of our group with a child, so we were all honorary aunts, even if I was pretty sure that none of us knew what we were doing in that regard.

Dakota was the brilliant one among us where that was concerned. We were all just flailing about, hoping we knew how to make our way.

"Hey there," I said, kneeling so I could hug him tightly. I didn't have to crouch as far down as I used to. The little boy was getting bigger and bigger with each passing day. A little clutch found its way into my belly, and I looked at Dakota, who seemed to know exactly what I was talking about.

"He just moved into a new size of clothing," Dakota said, her mouth dry. "I mean, soon, he's going to be taller than all of us."

"No, I'm not, Mom. You guys are always going to be bigger than me. Because you're the mom. And the aunts. I'm just a kid," he said, a long-suffering sigh in his voice.

I ran my hands through his hair, messing it up just a bit, and he kissed me on the cheek, smelling like little boy and apples. He must have just had his allotted amount of apple juice for the day. He loved the stuff, but there was so much sugar in it, even if Dakota found the healthiest version of it, he still wasn't allowed as much as he wanted. Considering that I wanted to bury myself in apple tarts, I felt for the kid.

"I'm so glad that I got to see you today," I said.

"I'm glad that you're here, too," he said solemnly and then went to the other women, skipping around, showing them his toys. After, he went back to the book sitting on the couch and proceeded to read to himself in quiet.

"I'm exhausted," Paris said, and I laughed.

"Seriously?" I asked.

"Seriously. I don't know how you do it every day, Dakota. But that one time I babysat for a whole evening? I had to take the next day off to recuperate."

"That's a lie," Dakota said, shaking her head as she kept her gaze on her son. "It is not. You're Superwoman, and I'm a little jealous." Paris paused. "Maybe not about the whole having to actually give birth thing because that scares me like nothing else, but I'm still jealous."

"He's the best thing that's ever happened to me," Dakota said, an odd twinge in her voice that I caught and thought the others might have, as well, but none of us asked about it in that moment. Dakota's secrets were her own. The girls knew about my ex, knew that I had been through hell, but we didn't discuss it at length. I knew I could if I needed to, but I never wanted to.

Dakota continued. "Now, let's pop open some champagne and sparkling apple juice and begin this brunch," Myra said, holding two bottles in her hands.

"Apple juice?" Joshua asked, and Dakota sighed.

"One glass of sparkling apple juice. You already had your regular apple juice for the day."

Myra winced and mouthed the word, *sorry*.

Dakota just shook her head. "No worries," she said, and sounded like she meant it.

"And you can have your sparkling juice in your cup with the lid because you're going to your playroom. Is that all right?" she asked.

"Because I might be a big boy, but big boys still spill," Joshua said, saying the words by rote as if he had heard and said them a thousand times before. I wouldn't be surprised if he had.

I laughed with the others as he got his cup, lid and all, and made his way to his room.

Dakota tapped the monitor in front of her. "I can watch him. That way, he has some privacy of his own while we have ours because I want to be able to talk freely about a certain date of yours," she said to me.

"I'll go read with Joshua," I said, and Paris gripped my arm, really tight.

"I'm not going to run away," I said honestly.

"Sure, you are," Paris said. "But that's good. I'll just chain you here if needed."

My pulse raced, and she looked at me and cursed under her breath.

"Fuck. I'm sorry."

"No, no. It's fine."

He hadn't used chains. It had been rope. It didn't matter, however, because none of that could touch me now. Not physically or mentally.

Just because the girls didn't know about the recent text, or the fact that he was out of jail, didn't mean that I had to talk about it now. I was fine.

If I kept saying that word, maybe I would actually believe it.

"Anyway, my date with Cross went well. We kissed," I

said, changing the subject. I knew I was throwing my love life into the fray so they wouldn't ask about Thomas, but I didn't want to talk about him.

I couldn't.

"I know you're changing the subject, but I'll allow it because I really want to know about the date," Paris said quickly.

"So, how was the kiss?"

"Amazing," I said, my voice a little breathy.

The girls swooned a bit, and I laughed.

"Seriously? No wonder we need this date pact. I said a kiss was amazing with no actual adjectives or descriptors, and it made all of you guys give me *that* look. You really do need dates."

"That's why we made the pact." Myra threw up her hands. "However, you were first. So we're going to need details. Lots and lots of delicious details."

"We ate our weight in sushi first," I said, and Myra just shook her head. "I swear, you and your sushi."

"What? It's good. And it's not like I had onions. So, no onion breath."

"No, just raw fish breath," Dakota said wryly.

"Maybe. But I really wasn't caring about that when his lips were on mine," I said. I was surprised that I was even going into this much detail, but these were my friends, and I needed to talk it out. I was holding so much in these days. Sometimes, things slipped. And I trusted them. I knew I should trust them with everything, and maybe that day would come, but this would do for now.

"Are you going to see him again?" Dakota asked.

"Of course, she is," Paris said. "Because she wouldn't walk away from something like this for anything. Right?" Paris asked.

"I, uh, yeah. But we haven't made plans yet. I'm in the middle of a busy semester and research. I already had this time scheduled off, but I should really be home grading."

"We're all busy," Dakota said. "In fact, let's get eating because I need to head back to the café after this. But that doesn't matter. As I said, we're all busy, but we're making time for us, and you're making time for Cross."

"You *are* going to try and make time for him, right?" Myra asked.

"Yes, I'm going to try."

"Why do you sound so resigned about that?" Paris asked.

I didn't say anything. Wasn't sure I could.

"Tell us more about him." We all looked at Dakota. "What? He's part of this now, even though he's not the guy we set you up with at first."

"No, he's better." My eyes widened at Paris's words. "Sometimes, I do make mistakes."

I clutched my hand over my heart. "No. Shocking."

Paris laughed. "Oh, shush. Let me just say that if I do make mistakes, they sometimes end up with the best results. After all, you met Cross because of me."

"I met Cross because his coworker is an asshole, and a little girl lost her appendix. That's not the best way to meet someone."

"But it is a way," Myra said honestly. "So, what does he do again?"

I explained about Chris Cross Furniture, and they all nodded. "Mother and Father have a few pieces from him. He's quite talented," Myra said.

I vaguely remembered that. "I had heard of him even before he went into detail about what he did. He's an artist."

"I will never understand paying that much for furniture," Dakota said, her gaze on the video stream where she watched her son play. "However, that's probably because I grew up differently than you guys."

I didn't feel bad about the fact that I had grown up with money or that I still had it. And Dakota wasn't trying to make me feel bad at all. She was just stating the truth. We all came from different walks of life, but we were friends now. And that was all that mattered.

"I want something from him now," Paris said. "I probably can't afford it, but I'm sure we could get the friends' discount. I mean, you are going to be sleeping with him, after all."

"Seriously? You're going to whore me out for a piece of furniture you don't even know you want?" I asked, levity in my tone.

"I do what I have to," Paris said, her eyes dancing with laughter.

"You haven't even seen his work," Myra said.

"If your parents have some, it's stunning. Right?"

"Oh, it is that, but I'm pretty sure they bought the most pretentious piece of art he's ever made," Myra said dryly.

"That is probably true," I said, laughing.

Myra's parents were not the best people. They regularly put others down and did their best to control her life. The fact that Myra was in Colorado with me now, rather than back in California where we had grown up, was a testament to that.

However, her family had phenomenal taste.

"Cross Brady does exquisite work," I said, "but you're not going to whore me out to get it."

"Brady?" Myra asked. "His last name is Brady?"

I frowned. "Yeah. Didn't I mention that?"

Myra shrugged, a different cool composure sliding over her face. What the hell was that about?

"I just hadn't put two and two together. I mean, I know his art, but I always thought of Chris and Cross, not Cross Brady. Anyway, you skimmed over the fact that you haven't slept with him yet. But you're going to, right? And not for furniture. I'll buy my own. I'll even get Paris a knickknack or something. However, tell us, are you going to sleep with him?"

I wanted to ask what Myra was thinking because she was definitely thinking something, but I didn't. Like I said before, we all had our secrets, and our own odd ways.

But it did kind of worry me that she had gone so pale at the mention of Cross's last name.

"I don't know if I'm going to sleep with him yet," I said.

"Are you going to tell us exactly how long it's been?" Paris asked, and I flipped her off. She just laughed, and Dakota put her hands over her face, while Myra rolled her eyes.

"Long enough that I actually said yes to this pact. And when and if I sleep with Cross, that'll be my business. I just don't know. We're taking it really slow. And I kind of like that."

They all looked at me, soft smiles on their faces.

"You sound different when you talk about him."

I frowned at Dakota. "I don't even really know him."

"You met him under weird circumstances, you still talk with him, and you're talking about him now. You just sound...different. And I'm not putting any pressure on you to do anything with or about him, but just know that I like you looking happy. We all need that, and I'm glad that you were the first to start finding that kind of happiness."

I looked at them as they continued talking to me about Cross, and I wondered what they saw. *Was* I happy? I didn't know. I enjoyed spending time with him, liked thinking about him. But it still made me nervous. I didn't know what I wanted out of this pact, out of what I had with Cross. But I was enjoying the journey.

At least, I thought so.

I'd thought I was happy before, and I had been so wrong.

I really didn't want to be wrong again.

We brunched, talked a bit more about Cross, and then work and our daily lives. Joshua came in to eat with us, and we chatted about school and friends and girls. He giggled because his best friend was a girl, and Dakota put her hands in front of her face and groaned.

Children were fun, but I was really glad that I didn't have any yet.

I went home soon after we finished because I had been honest when I'd said that I should have been grading.

I had my empty plate with me because even though the pastry had been store-bought, everything else had been homemade, and we had finished every single tart. I was full, probably a little bloated, and on a sugar high.

It was going to be fun working until I crashed.

I did my normal security routine when I got home, locked the doors, checked the windows, looked at my feed, and then slid off my shoes. I got a nice glass of water and a cup of tea and then went to see how long it would take me to get grading.

The text came about twenty minutes later, and I froze.

Had Thomas known I hadn't been home this whole time? Or was it just coincidence?

Unknown: *I miss you.*

Those words. Cross had said them in a text once, even though it had been a joke between us because we had just talked. And I hadn't felt like *this*.

The girls said those words all the time, and it didn't feel like this.

The words now sent my tea straight up my throat again, and I vomited everything I had eaten during brunch.

My hands shook, my whole body felt clammy, and I rechecked my security, then held my phone close to me.

I knew I needed to call the detective, like I had before. Because this could be Thomas. Or it could be Thomas's friends. He'd relied on them in the past to help him and I wouldn't put it past them and their money to do this—even if they'd cut him off when he'd gone to jail.

I didn't know.

Thomas was out.

Even though I had built my security around me, a bubble that I had hoped nothing could penetrate, I knew it wouldn't be enough.

It would never be enough when it came to Thomas.

As I hung up the phone after talking with the detective, getting empty assurances that they would help me, that they would do their best to protect me, I wondered if taking myself out of my comfort zone and trying with Cross was too much.

Because I had made a mistake before.

What if I was making one again?

Chapter 10

CROSS

I WAS RUNNING LATE. BUT THEN AGAIN, WHEN MY head was in the game, and I was enjoying my work, I tended to be focused on only that. However, people were waiting for me. Or, rather, *she* was waiting for me. I wasn't actually going to be late, but I did have to hurry up and finish what I was doing.

The project in front of me was complete, thank God. I was just going over it for anything I needed to change or work on before my clients picked it up. I felt like I'd done a good job, even if it wasn't my most elegant piece. I was still nervous about what the clients would think of the finished product, but that was always the case. No matter what I did, I was always nervous, even if it was damn good work.

I rolled my shoulders back, gave the piece one more nod, and then went on to the next item on my checklist before I could leave.

I went to my desk rather than my workroom and opened the files on my computer.

I really didn't want to do this, but I had to. I needed to go through every single one of my files, both those for my work and Chris's.

I needed to dissolve this partnership, and I had to make sure that everything was sound before I did. I did not want to fuck this up more than it already was, but this wasn't the first time I had gone over this paperwork in the past two days. Wasn't even the second. And I didn't like what I was seeing.

I had made a grave mistake. I'd trusted the wrong person. If I weren't careful, I was going to pay for it and with more than just a potential ulcer, and lack of sleep.

Chris was stealing from me. There was no getting around that, not when I looked at the numbers in front of my face.

I wouldn't have figured it out until I sat down and worked through every single error that I encountered. I wasn't even sure my accountant would have noticed it because he wouldn't have known that some of the items on the list were lies. He would have trusted me to make sure I sent him the right info, and would have trusted Chris to do the same. He would have double-checked everything, but there were some things that the accountant couldn't triple-check unless he knew the specifics behind every single item.

Even I was having trouble finding the reasons for some of these things, and I should have known every single one. This was my fault. I had fucked up by not looking sooner, and now I would have to figure out what the fuck to do. Should I go to the cops? Or to the IRS?

Because if this was fucked up the way it was, it likely wasn't the only thing. I had a feeling that Chris was fully aware of what was going on. We could potentially lose the business, and I would be the one on the hook when it came to the IRS. Because I didn't think Chris would be the one holding the bag at the end. No, he was going to leave that with me. He'd make sure of it.

"Fuck."

I went through the books line by line again, my back aching as I found myself twisted over my desk, wondering what the hell I was going to do. I had to be wrong.

I was just overthinking things.

"And that was how you got into trouble to begin with," I said.

By trusting the wrong person.

I saved everything and put it in my cloud so I could show Liam later. Liam would know what to do. And even though it grated on me that I would have to ask my brother-in-law for help, I knew that Liam would know who to talk to. I was grateful that I had someone to go to at all.

But, fuck. There was something wrong with what I was looking at, though I couldn't pinpoint the exact errors. And that meant I needed help. Because if the business went belly-up because of Chris, I didn't want to take the fall with him. And I wanted my fucking money.

I had bled for that, worked long hours for it, put every single ounce of myself into it. And Chris was stealing from me.

"Knock, knock," Chris said from the doorway. "You look so serious. What's wrong?"

I fisted my hands on the desk. I knew that this wasn't the time to go over everything. I didn't have all of the evidence ready, and I didn't even know what to say. Plus, I didn't know how Chris would react. What I wanted to do was wipe that smile from his face and beat the shit out of him. And since that wasn't the appropriate response, I didn't say anything. But, hell, we were about to have our reckoning, and it was a long time coming.

"Just going over some paperwork."

Was I wrong, or did I see a flash of fear on the other man's face? Maybe it was just cunning. Regardless, I saw too much.

"Oh." A pause. "New clients?"

Chris walked over to my side, and I closed the files, but not quickly enough.

"Accounting? That's not your job. Were those my files, too?" Chris rolled his shoulders back and glowered. "Going over my work? Or are you just jealous that I'm making more than you?"

"We know that's not the fucking case," I blurted, and then could have rightly hit myself upside the head.

Hadn't I just told myself that I was going to wait until I had all the evidence, that I was going to be cool and collected and not fuck things up? I sighed internally. I was so glad that I followed my own advice.

"Really? You're doubting me? We've worked together for how long? Well, fuck you, too. I'm sorry you're jealous of everything I can do and the people that I've brought in, but that's no reason for you to go through my accounts. How do I know you haven't touched any of my stuff? Have you stolen my clients while you're at it? Or maybe my accounts?"

"You've got to be fucking kidding me," I growled.

"What? You don't think I see you wanting what I

have. I was trying to throw you a bone with that client of mine, but hell, you couldn't even get that right."

The man had officially lost his fucking mind. He was twisting the truth as if I hadn't just lived through it.

What else had I been missing over the years because I had wanted to believe in what we'd once had?

I had wanted to believe that my trust had been earned.

I was so fucking wrong, and now I would pay the price. Maybe for a long damn time.

"You know what, I'm done. I've got shit to do, and I'm really not in the mood to deal with this."

"You're going to be in the mood to deal with this when I go through the paperwork myself."

I was grateful that I had already sent myself a copy because I was not in the mood handle or face whatever lies Chris came up with now. Our accountant had a copy, as well, and that would have to be enough for now. But hell. This was not what I had planned on doing today.

"You know what, I'm late. But you and I? We're going to have to talk soon."

"You keep saying that. Talk, talk, talk. And yet you don't do anything. You're just a sorry excuse for a man, and not the one I used to know. I'm pretty sure this partnership will be over soon."

"You know what? Fine. I wanted to dissolve it

anyway, but I was trying to figure out a good way to say that to you. Now, fuck it. We're going to have that talk soon. Because you and me? We're done. But it's not going to be as easy as you just walking away."

Chris looked at me, that fear in his gaze again. This time, I knew it wasn't just my imagination.

"Fuck you. You're going to regret saying that."

And then Chris was gone, and I wondered who the hell the man was. That wasn't the guy I had gone to school with. Wasn't the friend I had opened a business with. Who was the guy I was looking at now?

And here I was, the fucking loser still attached to him because I'd wanted to give him the benefit of the doubt.

How the hell was I supposed to even look at myself in the mirror at this point?

I didn't have time to wallow, though. No, I had a date.

A date with a woman that I had a feeling was a little scared of what was happening between us.

I probably should have canceled. I should have just walked away and let her have her space while I figured out what the fuck was going on.

But the selfish part of me didn't want that.

That part of me was afraid that if I did, there'd be no going back. I'd had those fears for long enough.

I got ready in a blur and nearly sped to the restaurant where I was meeting Hazel. I honestly wasn't sure that I should be on this date, but I wasn't going to cancel and be a jackass. I parked, noticed Hazel's car already there, and cursed under my breath. I hated that she was waiting for me. Hell, I needed to get my head on straight if I was going to do this. She deserved more than me being an idiot.

I also didn't mind that she'd met me at each of these dates. There was clearly something in her past, and secrets that she needed to keep. And I was fine with that. Maybe she'd trust me enough to tell me one day. If meeting me at a restaurant made her feel safe, then that was fine with me. I wasn't the type of guy who refused to listen, who imagined myself a caveman who could just get what I wanted by shouting and beating my fists against my chest.

Although I did kind of want to do that with Chris, but that was a completely different situation.

"Hey there," Hazel said from the bench near the doorway when I walked in.

I leaned down and brushed a kiss against her lips. My shoulders immediately relaxed, and I kept my eyes open enough to notice that hers did the same.

Hell, that was a good feeling. The tension eased from me, and I felt like I was coming home. Such a weird feeling for someone that I was still getting to know.

I didn't know what that meant, but what I did know

was that I wanted to push all of my other worries from my brain and only focus on her.

"I'm sorry I'm late. Work things that I can talk about later."

She just smiled.

"I don't mind. But I'm glad you showed up." She rolled her eyes and whispered, "They wouldn't let me get a table unless you were here."

"I have reservations," I said. "You should have been able to sit."

"Apparently, she didn't believe that I was actually with you."

I glowered and then looked over at the hostess, who had the grace to flush.

"I have no idea what that was about. But, fuck her," I whispered.

"I think that's kind of what she wants," Hazel said, her voice completely dry. I laughed, throwing my head back, my whole body shaking.

"Thank you for that. I needed to laugh." I kissed her again, then we made our way to the hostess stand. "Hi, Brady party of two," I said.

The hostess blinked at me but kept a smile on her face. "Right this way."

Apparently, everybody was going to gloss over the fact that she hadn't treated Hazel politely, even though I knew for a fact that there wasn't a policy that kept Hazel from taking a seat. In fact, my family came here often, and none of us ever arrived at the same time.

Well, that was fine. We weren't going to have to worry about that much longer.

Because now it was just us, and this date was something I craved. Just like I longed for Hazel.

That should worry me. But it didn't. She was a touchstone. One I hadn't been prepared for.

We took a seat, and the waiter came right away, taking our drink orders.

"This is quite an upscale place," Hazel said, looking around. "I've never been here before. I'll need to tell Myra about it. She loves foodie places."

I smiled. "It is a bit foodie for my family, but we like to come here for celebrations. And considering there are five of us, there's always a birthday or a promotion or something that we want to celebrate. But this is our place."

"It looks wonderful. And I'm kind of excited to try everything."

"Miss Noble?" an older gentleman said as he walked towards our table, a woman with a double strand of pearls at her throat and a skintight dress standing next to him.

I raised my brow. The cultured tone of the man's voice spoke of money, and the way he dismissed me with a casual glance spoke of snobbery. Or maybe I was just seeing too much into things after my dealings with Chris.

"Mr. Peterman. It's wonderful to see you," Hazel said in a completely different voice, one that I had never heard from her before. She sounded cultured, and a bit snobbish, as well.

Who the hell was *this* Hazel?

"I didn't know you were back in town. I haven't seen you around the vineyards in Napa recently. I should've known that you had moved out here."

"It's been a few years, Mr. Peterman. Mrs. Peterman, I presume?" she asked, nodding to the woman. Hazel didn't push back her seat to stand up, and neither did I. This was all so weird.

"Hello," the woman said, but didn't say anything else.

Well, then.

"Anyway, I see you're on a date," the man said, a questioning tone in the word *date*.

I should've been insulted by that, but I really didn't give a shit. I had my own problems to deal with. I didn't care what this asshole thought of me. I might not look like I had money, but I did. And I worked my ass off for it. No one needed to judge me for that. And even if I didn't have money, fuck him. Seriously. Fuck him hard.

"It's good to see you. I hope you have a wonderful night. I shall get back to mine."

If my brows could rise any farther on my forehead, they would be in my hair.

"Ah. It's good to see you out and about after, well... you know."

Hazel's expression completely shut down, and I wanted to kick the man's ass.

"Yes. Have a good night."

And then she turned from him, giving the other man what I thought I remembered one of my friends, Aaron, calling *the cut direct*.

Well.

That was interesting.

"Sorry about that," Hazel said, her cheeks completely pale. The waiter came by and dropped off her wine and my beer. She drank half her glass in one large gulp before we even had a chance to toast or anything.

Fuck.

"You want to talk about it? Or do you want to go? We can hit up a bar and get some wings and beer. Or I can follow you home to make sure you're safe."

Fear danced in her gaze, and I cursed myself. "Or I can not follow you home and not sound like a creep."

"I'm sorry. I'm sorry." She pinched the bridge of her nose and took a deep breath.

"There are a couple of things you should probably know about me. First, I'm not that person anymore, so you don't need to worry about me. Truly. I just need to breathe. It's just that I didn't expect to see him here. I hate that man because of what he represents, but I also don't like making a scene. Now, I feel like I'm making a horrible scene anyway."

"You're not. But what's wrong?"

She let out a breath. "I don't really know how to say this without sounding snobby."

"Let me guess. You come from money?" I asked. Her eyebrows rose.

"That's one way to put it."

"What's another way to put it?"

"Honestly, that's the best way to put it. My parents were wealthy. Big W, all of that. I grew up affluently and ran in the circles my mother told me to. Myra ran in those same circles. That's actually how we met. Now, we're both here. And, yes, I still have my family's money, but I mostly live on what I make at the school. Which isn't much, but compared to what others make, it's great. I didn't live up to my family's expectations, but I'm used to that. However, that's pretty much what most little rich girls say."

"Hazel."

She waved her hand in front of her face and smiled, but it didn't reach her eyes. "Sorry. That's what my ex-husband used to say. Thomas."

Something turned in my gut. It wasn't jealousy. But I knew I wasn't going to like where this led.

"I'm going to need more wine for this, but I'm driving."

"We can leave your car here, and I can have one of my brothers pick it up."

"No, falling into a bottle won't help me either." She let out another breath, composing herself. She looked like a Valkyrie. Strong and fucking sexy. I admired her so much in this moment, but I couldn't say that. Not when I knew she was barely holding it together. "We married young. I was nineteen. Stupid and I didn't understand what I was getting into. But it was what my family wanted. Thomas was who my parents thought I needed to marry. He was old money, even older than the Nobles'."

"The way you say that sounds like you're from the Regency era."

"Our money's actually older than that," she said. And then she sighed. "But that doesn't matter. Honestly, I have the privilege of saying that. I donate what I can, and I actually pay my taxes, but yes, I have money. You do, too. But you earned yours."

"Hey, you work your ass off. You don't have to."

"I guess that's true. It's just a touchy subject. But back to my story. There I am, poor little rich girl—as I said, Thomas would say that when I wanted to work. When I wanted to fund things myself. Anyway, he was chosen for me, and I happened to fall in love with him. It was one of the worst mistakes of my life."

"You don't have to talk about this if you don't want to."

"I don't want to go into too much detail, mostly because we're in public, and I don't really want to talk about it, but I feel like I need to. Thomas was not a nice man. After my parents died, he didn't have his leash anymore. He hurt me in more ways than one. He was a horrible person. He stalked me when I left him. He hurt me. Over and over. And when he went to prison, it created a vast media nightmare, at least in our circles. That's what Mr. Peterman was referring to. He was surprised seeing me out and about because of the incident."

"Jesus. I don't know what to say. Are you safe now?"

"I don't know if I'll ever be safe with him out. And that's the honest truth. I don't know. But there's nothing I can do about it. I have security on my house. The detectives know what's going on." She shook her head when I opened my mouth to say more.

"I don't want to dive into it again. Just know I'm fine. I know it's a paltry word for what I feel, but it's the truth. I went through hell, and he caused it, though I caused a little bit because of my determination to do things on my own. I can't change that."

"Don't you dare blame yourself." Rage coursed through me, but I held it back. The thought of Hazel being hurt made me want to find Thomas and rip his head off his shoulders. But adding more violence to the situation wouldn't help anyone.

"I didn't like the fact that Mr. Peterman threw that in my face, but now I guess you understand a bit more of why I'm careful about who I meet. And why it's taken me so long to go out on a date again."

I reached across the table and touched her hand. She didn't pull away. Thank God. "You're so fucking brave. You don't need to tell me anything more. It's not my business to know. It's your right to tell me what you need to. But the fact that you're even going out again? I'm so proud of you. That the guy happens to be me? I'm one lucky son of a bitch."

I said the words a bit crudely to make her laugh, to jolt her out of wherever she was in her head just then.

I hated what she had been through, and I hated more that I couldn't change it. But I could be there for her. All thoughts of what I was dealing with in regards to Chris flew from my mind, and my inner overprotective asshole came back in full force.

"Let's just have a good night. Let's play foodie and eat

and drink the rest of this wine, and then maybe chug some water," she added with a laugh. "And let's pretend that everything is flowery and wonderful. Because that's what I need."

"I can do that. I can be that for you."

"Good. And then maybe you can tell me why you looked so glower-y even before I told you a bit about my past."

"I thought you said you wanted to have a good time."

"Cross."

I told her about work and Chris, and when she gripped her wine glass tightly and forced herself to set it down, her eyes narrowed in anger, I knew that I had been missing this.

I needed this. Having someone to talk to, to share my fears with. To just be with.

I hadn't been looking for Hazel. But I'd found her, just like she'd found me.

And as I thought about Chris and this Thomas asshole, I knew that things weren't perfect, but we were trying to find our way.

I didn't want to let Hazel go. Even though I was still getting to know her, I felt like I already knew her inside and out.

And that should scare me, but it didn't.

It just made me want her more.

And even more, it made me want to be a man who deserved her.

I could fall for her if I let myself. Fuck, maybe I already had.

And I had no idea what the hell to do about that.

Chapter 11

Hazel

Was I making a mistake? Perhaps. But it was my mistake to make. I could do this. I could let a man into my inner sanctum and not stress out.

My hands gripped the steering wheel even as I snorted at that thought. Talk about a double entendre when it came to the phrase *inner sanctum.*

Cross was behind me in his car, following me to my house. After this, he would know where I lived. I was going to let him inside.

What were we to do then? That was up to both of us once we got there. He told me more about himself. We had spent so long talking over dinner that we had closed down the restaurant.

I knew our waiter probably hadn't been happy with us taking up the table for so long, but we had compensated him with a nice tip.

But we had been just the two of us, me and Cross. We'd spent so much of our time together tonight learning about one another. I had told him about my past, and he hadn't run. No, he'd stayed. He'd been there for me. And he hadn't judged. He'd been angry on my behalf. And then he'd told me about his past, his worries.

And I'd been there for him.

All over drinks and dinner.

Baring our souls the barest of inches. Yet it was the start of something.

Something *new*. Something for now.

As he followed behind me and I drove home, I realized he would potentially be in my house.

"There's no potential about it," I told myself.

It had to be intentional. I had to take this step. I needed to not be so scared. I trusted him. And the thing was, I hadn't always trusted Thomas. Oh, I might've told myself that I had fallen head over heels for him, but he had been in my life because of my parents. I'd never once blamed them for what had happened, but I did blame myself for falling the way I did.

For ignoring the warning signs.

I didn't sense any red flags when it came to Cross. I had to hope that was enough.

I had to believe. I had to jump in. I had to...be.

I parked in my garage, and he pulled into the driveway. I shut the garage door behind me, having told him this part of my routine.

That he would have to wait for me to come around.

I let out a deep breath and then went through all of my security measures, looking at him through the security camera and putting my finger on the screen.

"Let's do this," I whispered.

And then I made my way to the door and opened it, having checked through the peephole and the camera on my phone again just in case.

I was probably being overly cautious, but I was letting someone into my house.

I needed this to work.

Shivers slid up and down my body, but it wasn't from fear. No, it was the look on Cross's face.

The dark one that told me he was thinking thoughts that went along the same path as mine, things that had nothing to do with security. But rather what walking over that threshold would mean for the both of us.

"May I come in?" he asked.

I took a step back, swallowing hard, unable to speak.

"You need to use your words, Hazel. I need to make sure. Don't be scared."

I smiled, knowing he was right. He was doing all the right things. That should worry me, but it didn't.

"Please come in, Cross."

And then he did.

I closed the door behind him, locking it securely, and then I let out a deep breath as I turned to him. I placed my palms on the door and leaned back, trying to breathe. I inhaled that woodsy scent of his and my toes curled. I loved it.

"So. This is my home."

Awkward, much?

It was probably larger than I needed, but it wasn't a McMansion or anything like that. However, because I sometimes had trouble leaving the house after everything that had happened with Thomas, I'd wanted an easily defensible place that was mine. Somewhere I wouldn't feel claustrophobic in if I didn't leave for days.

That was probably a weird thing to think, but they were my thoughts, so I went with it.

"It's nice." He let out a breath. "Hell, it's beautiful. Sorry, I told you before I wasn't good at this. Now, here we are, alone in your house. I know this is a momentous occasion, but all I want to do is kiss you."

I let out a breath. "Then let's not think about the

momentous occasion part. Let's not make this anything but normal. And why don't you kiss me?"

He raised a brow.

"Really?"

"Yes. Kiss me. And let's pretend everything is normal."

Cross let out a little laugh that wasn't entirely full of humor. "I don't think either one of us is normal. However, it is you and me. You tell me what you want."

"I don't know what I want, not in the grand scheme of things. But I do know I want you to kiss me now." I wanted to feel. I wanted to just be.

Cross took a step forward and slowly traced his finger along the line of my jaw. I leaned into him, resisting the urge to close my eyes. I wanted to watch him, to see every movement. And not because of fear. Because I wanted to soak in every single moment of time that I had with him.

I had found myself over time. The real me. I had figured out who I needed to be as I grew and healed.

Cross wasn't healing me. I had done that myself.

But now, I was finding who I could be when I wasn't alone. When I wasn't relying on just my strength.

I could imagine myself with someone else and not just in the vastness of my aching heart, in my soul, and its depth of loneliness.

But I didn't have to worry about any of that.

I could have him.

Finally. "Be sure."

In answer, I went up on my tiptoes and pressed my lips to his.

Luckily, he had lowered his head so I could do it easily, and I kept my eyes open, slowly parting my lips so I could kiss him deeper.

He grinned against my mouth and then slid his hand into my hair, tugging it ever so slightly.

Thomas had done that once and had pulled me across the floor, but this was different. I only had a vague memory of the pain of the past, and it didn't matter now.

Because I wasn't that person.

And Cross wasn't that man.

Instead, it was just him and me, and this feeling, this sensation.

Cross took a step back, only a small one so his hand could still cup my face, his mouth remaining close to mine.

"I like doing that," he whispered.

"I like you doing that. I think we need to do it again," I whispered. My eyes widened. "You make me want to say anything. I'm not always like this."

Cross tilted his head, running his hand over my hair. "I don't know about that. You've always said what you think when you're in front of me. And you did let me sit down the first night we met. And when you text me, you always call me out on my bullshit. I think that person's always been in there. I like the fact that you're showing her to me."

I looked up at him, a smile playing on my face. "I like that. It's a good thought. Is it true? I don't know. But I'd like to believe it's true."

"I should go now," Cross said, his voice low, but his eyes never leaving mine.

I swallowed hard. My hands weren't shaking now, but my voice was. "What if I don't want you to go?"

He studied my face, and I wanted to run my hands through his beard. "Are you sure you're ready for that?"

I licked my lips. His gaze moved with the motion. My nipples tightened, and my pulse raced. From just one look.

"I let you into my home, Cross. I don't think any other action or word would be a better example of what I'm ready for. Don't go. Not yet."

I wasn't usually this forward, this...dare I say, brazen. And I liked it. I liked who I was when I was with Cross. I enjoyed how I felt when I was without him, as well. As if he'd unlocked something within me that I just couldn't grasp. I loved it.

"I'm going to kiss you again."

"You have my permission to kiss me as many times as you want."

"Good."

And then his lips were on mine. This time, I let my eyes close and I sank into him, my hands trailing up his back, gripping his shoulders as his mouth devoured mine. He seemed to want more, and I wanted more, too. I needed more.

His lips trailed along my jaw, and I let my head fall back so he could kiss my neck, leaving shivers of sweet temptation all over my body.

My knees shook, and he led me towards the couch, slowly backing me up so my butt was against the back of the sofa, his mouth on mine.

Somehow, my jacket was on the floor, and my eyes were still closed. I wanted my mouth on his and my hands on his body. He was just so strong, so hard and broad.

Everything about him was muscle and strength. A man who knew exactly what he was doing with his hands.

"You taste amazing," Cross said, his fingers brushing my hair behind my shoulders.

"Really?" I had no idea what I was saying, I only knew that I wanted his hands and mouth on me. I wanted to hear his growl of a voice.

I just wanted *him*.

"Really. Now I want to taste you everywhere."

I should have blushed. I didn't. Instead, my hands went to the bottom of my shirt, and I pulled it up. His hands went to mine, stopped me for a moment. For a second, I thought maybe he didn't want this, that I was moving too fast. Instead, he kissed me again and helped me lift my shirt over my head. I stood there in my shoes and slacks and a bra, feeling far more naked than I actually was.

"Beautiful," Cross said, and then he moved to my breasts, kissing them, molding them. When he undid my bra, my breasts fell heavily into his palms. I reached back to hold onto the couch, my head tipping back. He laughed, kissing and gently biting.

He moved from one to the other, his body close to mine, hot, heated. I wanted more of him, but I loved that he was taking over, and I could just be.

I didn't know many other people I could do that with.

And then he dropped to his knees, and I swallowed hard, my legs shaking.

"Let me," he said. He took off my shoes, and then his hands were on my pants.

"Ready?"

"For you? Of course."

"Good." And as he tugged down my leggings, the fabric bunching over my butt as he pulled. I let out a shaky breath, finding myself bare except for the tiny scrap of silk on my body.

"Jesus Christ, I knew you had curves, I knew you were fucking sexy, but damn, Hazel. It's hard for me to breathe when I look at you."

I swallowed hard and looked down at him, his dark hair between my legs, and I almost came right then.

"What exactly are you going to do now?" I asked, nearly teasing.

Only there wasn't anything *nearly* about it.

"Exactly what you want me to do."

And then he was breathing hot air over my flesh and tugging my panties aside. His mouth was on my pussy, one leg thrown over his shoulder, the other keeping me steady as I gripped the back of the couch.

My body shook, and his tongue lapped, parting my flesh as he kissed me intimately. I heated from the inside out, my entire body trembling. When he played with my clit, a touch there, a touch here, and his finger slid into me, I couldn't hold back anymore. The sight of his dark hair against my pale skin was too much. I came, gasping, my nipples hard, a tingling sensation running up my spine.

The orgasm flooded me, encompassing me in warmth and racking me with shudders as I leaned against the couch.

Cross lapped up my orgasm, clearly wanting more. I

couldn't breathe, I didn't know what to do. And then he was on his feet again, his lips on mine. I came down from my high, tasted myself on his tongue, and tugged at his shirt. I needed more, craved it.

I had no words, but he seemed to know what I wanted. Thankfully, he knew exactly what I needed.

He took off his shirt, and I helped him with his pants as he toed off his shoes. We both laughed when he nearly fell over.

I didn't know there could be laughter with sex. I didn't know I needed it.

Suddenly, he was naked, his hot flesh in my hand as I squeezed the base of him.

He slid his hand over mine and groaned.

"You touch me like that, and I'm going to come right on those pretty breasts of yours."

My nipples tightened at the words. Those crass, vulgar words that were so fucking hot.

"And what if I want you to do that?" I asked.

He crossed his eyes, and I licked my lips.

"Maybe next time. And don't even think about putting that pretty, pouty mouth on my dick. I don't think I could handle it."

I pumped his shaft, my fingers not able to touch around his girth.

I honestly didn't know how he was going to fit, but I couldn't wait to try.

I squeezed my thighs together, aching for him, wondering who the hell this wanton woman was. This wasn't the Hazel Noble I had always known.

No, this was a Hazel who took chances. Who went on blind dates and had accidental ones. This was a Hazel who asked for what she wanted and made sure she got it.

This was the Hazel that had asked Cross over, the one that was going to ride this very large dick.

I squeezed him again and then ran my hand up his length so I could press my thumb to his slit, spreading his precum. His whole body shook against me, and the power I felt was like nothing I'd ever felt before.

"I need to get a fucking condom," he whispered. "Shit. It's in my car. I don't keep them in my wallet anymore."

I groaned and let out a little laugh. "You couldn't have thought of that before you got all naked, and I was holding your dick?" I asked.

"Hey, I couldn't help it. I really wanted you to hold my dick."

"Hold on right there," I whispered. And then I ran off, a laugh bursting free from my lips because I was bouncing everywhere. He just stood there, standing in my living room, completely naked.

I would've thought this might ruin the mood, but not

even a little. I went to my bathroom, pulled out a box of condoms, ripped it open, and spread the packages all over the floor, all the while continuing to laugh like I had lost my damn mind. I brought four of them with me into the living room.

Cross raised a brow, his gaze on my hand and then my breasts as I put my hands on them to keep them steady.

"Really? I'm not as young as I used to be. Maybe we can get through two. Perhaps three."

I froze, blinking. "I was just kidding with the number of condoms I grabbed." I paused. "Three times?" I asked, my voice really high-pitched.

"Fuck, yeah. Three times. If you want to get to four, though, I'll have to begin soon. Maybe stretch." He rolled his shoulders back, and then he lunged. I laughed and found myself on my back on the couch, his mouth on mine.

It took no time at all for him to bring me close to orgasm again, his hand between my thighs, rubbing me until I was panting, my hands on his back, wanting more.

And then he was sheathed in a condom, the sound of the wrapper an echo in my head, and I looked at him, trusting him more than I ever thought possible.

"Are you ready?" he whispered.

"I'm ready," I whispered back.

And then he was inside me, stretching me to the limit. I could barely breathe.

This was everything. *He* was everything. But I couldn't hold onto that, not right now.

I had to live in the moment. I just had to be.

But I could do this. This was what I needed. And I hadn't even known.

We were on the couch, and he could barely fit. It didn't matter because he was inside me, we were connected. And I wanted this. I *needed* this.

"You feeling good?" he asked.

"I feel everything."

He winked and then kissed me softly.

"Me, too."

And then he moved.

I moved with him, slightly unsure of what I was doing because it had been so long, but it didn't matter. Because this was right. We were right.

I arched into him, and he slid deeper. We both moaned, his dick touching me in just the right place inside.

And then he moved faster, harder, pounding into me, his hands on my hips, keeping me steady as he pumped.

I played with my breasts, arching for him, and then I was coming, clamping around his cock. A breath later, he was coming with me, shouting my name, and then leaning over me, his lips on mine as he continued to pound, continued to fill me.

After, he moved to the side, bringing me half on top of him, and half to the side on the couch. Both of us lay there panting, his dick still inside me, my body still shaking.

"Wow," Cross said, running his hands over my body.

"Agreed. Wow."

"I may have to shave, or I'm going to end up giving you beard burn," Cross said, slowly running his hands over my body again.

I tried to sit up, but it was hard when he was still inside. Instead, I pushed at his shoulder.

"What?" he asked.

"Don't you dare fucking shave. You already told me you have beard oils and take care of your facial hair to the point where it's cleaner than most people's hair."

"Of course. Germs. It's gross."

"Don't you dare shave it. You put enough conditioner in there that it's softer than my hair. You didn't give me beard burn. And, I like the scruff."

He smiled and kissed me again. "You like the beard?"

"Didn't I just say that?"

"Then I won't shave it. I'll keep it, which is a good thing because I really like my fucking beard."

I smiled and ran my hands over the facial hair in question, and then through his silky locks, and then down his body, coming to rest on his hips.

"Wow," I whispered.

"I'm going to take that as a compliment. And if you're lucky, I'm pretty sure round two's on its way."

My eyes widened, even as I laughed. Seriously? I didn't know you could laugh during sex like this.

"Really?"

"I'll need inspiration."

And then his hands were on my breasts, his lips on mine, and I laughed again, savoring the moment.

I had no idea what was coming next, but right then, I didn't care.

Because, somehow, I'd accidentally found this man, and I couldn't wait to just live in the moment some more.

I'd heard forever only happened once, but that was fine with me because I wasn't looking for forever.

I was looking for right now.

And I had found it.

The part of me that wanted more didn't want to let go, so I ignored that part and decided to just be.

After all, I had to find my happiness, too.

And that was more than any forever I could ever hope for.

Chapter 12

CROSS

THIS WAS IT. THIS WAS THE CULMINATION OF OVER A decade of friendship, and so many fucking issues that I could barely breathe.

I was finally going to end it.

The fact that it sounded like a relationship beyond what I had with Chris just told me that I had been in too deep with this business partnership and whatever friendship we'd had.

Because Chris wasn't my friend. He hadn't been for a long while, and the fact that I was just coming to realize that told me that I'd had rose-colored glasses on or my head down to the point where I was a fucking idiot. And anything that happened from here on out was something I would have to deal with.

I had talked with Liam and contacted a lawyer. We were going to dissolve the partnership, and I would see if I'd have to sue my former best friend.

But at the moment, I needed to make sure that we could talk for at least a few moments. I needed to ask him what the hell he'd been thinking. Chris wasn't violent, so I wasn't worried about that. And the accounts were locked down, so he couldn't fuck up anything there. At least not any more than he already had. But I wasn't going behind his back like he had done to me for so long. I needed to talk to him.

I had to make sure that I wasn't the one without a soul after this.

My lawyer had advised me against going into too much detail, and that was fine with me. I just needed to talk to Chris. I needed to see what he would say.

I'd deal with the rest later.

I didn't know what to do beyond that, but that would come.

Besides focusing on my failings at Chris Cross Furniture, and the fact that I actually still had work to do, I also had Hazel on my mind.

We'd had six dates. Six outings where I was getting to know her in every way possible.

I hadn't been expecting her, and I honestly didn't know if I should have expected her.

Everything about what we had was completely new to me, and I fucking loved it.

I was just trying to figure out exactly what the hell I was going to do about it.

With my professional life up in the air, going out with Hazel felt like a touchstone to me.

It also felt like, if I wasn't careful, I could fuck it up and hurt her more than she'd already been hurt.

I didn't know every detail of what had happened between her and her ex-husband. It wasn't my right to know until she was ready to tell me. However, despite not knowing the details, I wanted to find the asshole and murder him.

No, that was going a little too far. But I did want to kick his ass. How dare he hurt such a kind person? How dare he hurt anyone for that matter? I saw the shadows in her eyes when she spoke of him. How strong she tried to be as she rolled her shoulders back and pretended that she was fine. And while I knew she was better in every sense of the word she needed to be, there was nothing good about what the man had done.

But she trusted me. And that trust meant everything. I

had the trust of my family, the comfort of knowing that no matter what happened, they could lean on me and vice versa in case the worst ever happened.

I knew that when Arden was sick, she could come to me. When Prior's anxiety got to be too much, and he couldn't laugh through his issues, he could come to me. When Macon didn't want to talk but just wanted to sit and focus on what he needed to do, he could come to me. And when Nate kept his secrets, he knew he didn't need to tell me. I didn't need to know them unless he wanted to tell me. Regardless, he could and did always come to me.

My parents trusted me to be the head of the household when they moved away. And while I didn't begrudge them finding new jobs and a life that worked for them, I also realized I was fine being who I needed to be for them. Even if I was still figuring it out.

Despite all of that, I didn't know if I'd ever had anyone in my family truly see me as someone to lean on.

Hazel trusted me. She trusted me with where she lived, with her body, and maybe, if I got deep about it, her heart.

Hell, for someone who needed to have control and to be protective of everyone around them, the fact that she did that for me meant that I couldn't fuck this up. I couldn't be so focused on my work that I hurt her.

And I'd be damned if I ever hurt her. Thomas had

hurt her physically and emotionally. That wasn't going to be me. No matter what.

I didn't know what would happen between us, didn't even know what I wanted from the relationship. I sure as hell hadn't been looking for her when we crossed paths, but it'd happened, and I wasn't going to take it for granted.

First, however, I had to deal with whatever the fuck was going on with work.

The door opened to the building, and I muttered to myself, "Speak of the devil."

"Cross? I saw your truck. You here?"

I had brought the truck because I needed to move a few pieces of equipment around, so I had parked in the back. Apparently, Chris had driven around the building, saw I was here, and parked in the front. Hell.

"I'm in my office." I locked up my computer as well as all the files just in case, and then walked out the door.

What was I going to say to him? I honestly wasn't sure. I didn't have a plan in my head. Maybe I shouldn't say anything.

But as I looked at Chris's crisp shirt, his hands that hadn't seen a piece of wood in months, hadn't held a sander or varnish or anything having to do with what we did when we had built this place from the ground up, I wondered who the fuck this person was. And how I had let my own desires of making this place work tarnish the memory of what we'd had.

I really wasn't good at relationships. I had told Hazel that before.

But I clearly wasn't good at friendships either. Because I had ignored all the warning signs for far too long. And now I had to deal with the consequences. Consequences that had cost me way too much fucking money and time.

"Hey," Chris said. "I saw you were here. Thought I'd stop by."

"It's working hours. Of course, I'm here."

And you're not.

Chris's eyes narrowed. "Anyway, I have a couple of meetings today to figure out exactly what I'm going to do with this huge piece coming up. You know, the great commission?"

The lie? There was no commission. Just Chris wining and dining and trying to use our name to get money. It made no sense in our business. You actually had to create goods in order to get something.

"Anyway, I just wanted to see what you were up to. Anything you're working on, on the side?"

Like pieces he could sell for me and make a large commission on? That wasn't going to happen. But it had happened. A couple of pieces that I hadn't done for a commission but had finished in the past. A couple of years ago, Chris had sold them for us because he'd had the connections. I hadn't minded because I was working on the next thing, focused on my work. I had thought I had the receipts to know how much I'd made. I had been wrong. Chris had been stealing from me this whole time. And I had been too fucking trusting to actually realize it.

Or, I had actually believed the documentation and hadn't noticed that it was fabricated. A legit lie.

The man had broken the law, and I hadn't even noticed.

Who the fuck was I?

"No, I'm good. Working on projects that are already spoken for."

"Too bad," he said, and I narrowed my eyes. "Chris, we need to talk."

He didn't take a step back, but his eyes narrowed. "So I hear."

"Excuse me?" I asked, tension running up my spine.

"I hear you went to a lawyer. You can't even talk to me? No, you keep saying you want to talk, but you've got too small of a dick to actually lay it all out there. You want out of this partnership? Fine. I can see that you've never thought you could live up to what I can make anyway. But don't you fucking think you can spread lies about me. That is slander. Libel."

The two words did not mean the same thing, like Chris was saying, but I wasn't going to correct his grammar.

Right then, all I wanted to do was punch him in the face. But I'd just told myself that I wasn't a violent person. I couldn't do that.

"Really, Chris? That's the line you're going with?"

"What? What other lines are there? You want to leave this business because you think you're too good for me. But I'm the one raking in the big deals. I'm the one making art for celebrities. You're just whittling in the corner for some mom and pop shop, wondering why the fuck you're not living the life you should. I tried to throw you a bone, and you did nothing."

"Throw me a bone? With that meeting? At 59th? Hell, you couldn't even do that right."

I let out a breath, trying to calm myself. "I seriously cannot fucking believe you right now. That was your client. And she canceled."

He narrowed his eyes. "Because she knew she wouldn't be able to work with you."

"And that's just a fucking lie. All you fucking do is lie."

"No, you're the one who lies to yourself. I've always been the better artist. I took pity on you because your name worked for what I wanted to do. But now? You think you can just walk away. Fine, we'll make that work. You can walk away, but Chris Cross is mine."

"No, that's not how this works. That's not how the partnership is laid out."

"We'll see what my lawyer says about that. Because fuck you and all the lies you're spreading. Fuck you, thinking that you can do whatever you want and pretend that you're anywhere close to my talent. I've always been better than you. I've always made sure that you had the little things that you needed to get things done. But you are nothing. You've always been nothing. You'll always *be* nothing. I'm the artist. I'm the one people will remember. You're just a guy with the weird fucking name and the big fucking family. You're the one who takes too much time off so you can go take care of your sick little sister. Just because she married rich and doesn't need you to take care of her anymore so she doesn't die, doesn't mean you can suddenly spend all your time here."

I didn't even know I had moved in front of him, my fist ready to slam into his face, until it was done. Chris's nose crunched from the power of my punch, and I cursed.

Apparently, I *was* a violent man.

"You're going to pay for that, you fucking asshole. Wait until you hear from my lawyer. You'll be lucky if you're not in a jail cell tonight. Asshole."

Chris stormed out, his hand over his face as blood

poured down. I pinched the bridge of my nose, my knuckles aching, wondering what the fuck I was doing.

I had just hit a man. I knew the repercussions would come.

And, fuck, I now had to go to my house where Hazel would be. Have her see that, yes, I had just hit a man. There would be no hiding it, because my hand would be aching later.

I had hit a man, and she didn't deal with violence well.

She shouldn't have to.

I guess I deserved exactly what I got after this.

My hands shook, and I closed up the place, somehow making it to my house without throwing up or driving off the road.

Fuck. Knowing Chris, he was probably going to sue me. Or I'd end up in jail for hitting him. But the fucking asshole had talked about Arden. He didn't have the right to talk about my baby sister. Nobody did, especially not a fucking asshole who was going to use her sickness for his own gains. But for what? To make himself feel better about himself? Fuck that.

Anger still coursed through my veins as I pulled into the driveway and cursed at myself again when I saw Hazel's car there.

I pulled up next to her, and she waved, a smile on her face. I got out, taking deep breaths to calm myself.

"Hell, I'm late."

"Actually, I'm early. There was like no traffic on 36, and I'm not exactly sure how that happened. But, here I am." She leaned forward, kissed me softly, and I leaned into the touch, needing more.

She pulled back and looked at me, frowning.

"What's wrong?"

"Nothing."

"I don't think you've ever lied to me before. But that was definitely a lie."

Then she looked down at my hand, the redness on the knuckles evident because I had hit the guy pretty hard, and her eyes widened.

"What happened?" she whispered.

"I hit Chris. I'm so sorry." Jesus, I was an asshole. I shouldn't even touch her with these hands.

Her eyes widened, and she took my hand in hers, brushing her fingers over my bruised knuckles. It didn't hurt, I had punched a punching bag enough that it wouldn't, but the fact that she cared for me like this? I wasn't sure exactly what to think.

"Why are you apologizing to me? What happened exactly?"

"Let's get you inside," I said, tucking a strand of hair

behind her ear. She didn't flinch. That had to count for something.

"Unless you want to leave."

She frowned again. "Why would I want to leave? I need you to tell me." And then her eyes widened, and she cursed. I kind of liked it when she swore. It was hot.

"What happened to me and what you and Chris probably just dealt with are two separate things. I know not everybody has the same experiences as I did, and not everyone would react the same if they went through similar experiences to mine. However, I know you. I know you're not violent. Let's go inside. I'll take care of your hand, and you can tell me what happened with Chris. I knew you were going to talk with him today, but I didn't know it was going to be an all-out confrontation."

My heart hammered in my chest, and I leaned down and pressed my lips against hers. I knew my beard rubbed against her chin, and she smiled because I knew it sometimes tickled her.

"I don't know what I did to deserve you," I whispered.

She blinked, her eyes filling for a moment before that went away as if I had imagined it.

"I don't know why you think you don't deserve me," she whispered, and then I sighed and let her into the house.

"So," I whispered.

"Come on, let's ice your hand."

"It doesn't hurt."

"It'll give me something to do because all I want to do is baby you and make you feel better, and I'm really not good at that. If you can't tell, I'm really only nurturing when it comes to my students, and even then, I'm not very good at it."

I laughed softly.

"I'm really not good at this either," I said honestly.

"You don't have to be," she said.

"Now, tell me what happened."

I went through it all, and her eyes narrowed as I kept talking, her cheeks pinking with what I hoped was anger. Or maybe embarrassment for me. After all, I had hit someone today.

"That fucker."

I barked out a laugh. "Really?"

"Why wouldn't it be really? I cannot believe him. That is such a lie to try and save face. I can't believe he would say that about Arden. I mean, I've only seen her on FaceTime, but she seems like a wonderful person, and she doesn't deserve whatever he said about her. Hell, I want to hit him, too. And we know I'm never going to hit anybody. Not after what happened."

The fact that she could say anything like that floored me.

"Maybe," I whispered.

"Thomas was more emotionally abusive to me than anything. He belittled me, made me feel like I was nothing. He took my phone when I wasn't listening to him. He cut me off from friends. I didn't speak to Myra for my entire marriage because he thought she wasn't good enough for me. My best friend wasn't good enough. He cut me off from Paris even during school, so she thought I was a stuck-up bitch, even though he was the one that said *she* was. He did all of that, and I didn't realize it until it was too late. He slapped me on my stomach and my thighs when I wasn't skinny enough for him. He pulled me by my hair that one time, but never again because I flinched in public afterwards.

"He did all of that, and I hadn't even realized he was doing it until it was too late. I became a statistic, and I didn't even realize it. When I finally went to the cops, thankfully, they believed me. He'd told me over and over again that they would never believe me. He blamed me, just like Chris is blaming you now. It took a lot of therapy. It took a ton of talking and realizing who I was. I'm here now, and while I can never see myself hitting someone, maybe I could. To protect someone I love, maybe I could. But Chris deserves to go to jail. He doesn't deserve any more of your time, and hopefully, no more of your thoughts."

I looked at her then and cupped her face, wondering how the hell I found myself here with her. It made no sense to me. Not when I had spent so many years alone, making sure that everybody around me was safe and had what they needed. I hadn't thought of myself.

"I want to find Thomas, and I want to hurt him. And that makes me feel like a horrible person," I said, not wanting to hide that from her.

"Small parts of me want to hurt him, too," she said, and I leaned forward, resting my forehead against hers as she iced my knuckles.

"I don't know what that says about me that I want to retaliate. But in the end, I just want to be left alone."

"Has he texted you since those first two times?"

She had finally told me about that, and I had seen such rage in her as she relayed the story that I wanted to wrap her in bubble wrap and take her back to my house, along with the rest of my family, where I could create a fort and no one could hurt us.

It was unreasonable, but sometimes, I got unreasonable for those I loved.

I froze. Loved? Wow, that was a new word. One I wasn't ready to focus on.

"He hasn't texted again. The detectives say he's where he needs to be, back in California. That he isn't anywhere close, and he's checking in with his parole officer. He isn't near me. And he can't hurt me. They can't trace the texts to him. We don't even know if it was him. However, I don't want to live in fear, and I don't want to live in anger. Therefore, I'm living in whatever emotion I have left."

I leaned forward and ran my lips across hers.

"Thank you," I whispered.

She frowned.

"For what?" she asked.

"For being you. For reminding me that my life isn't the out-of-control weirdness of work or whatever the fuck Chris is doing. You're here. And you're pretty fucking amazing."

"Between work and the date pact that is going nowhere with the others for now, thank you for making my part easy."

I laughed and then kissed her, slowly at first until it deepened into something more.

We were in my kitchen, the two of us mired in so many emotions I knew we should probably slow down, but we didn't. Instead, she raised her hands and let me strip off her shirt, slowly, until my hands were on her breasts. My lips there, too. Her hands slid down my back, cupping, grasping, and then we were both naked, her on the kitchen counter, and me standing there before her. When she slid the condom over my dick, squeezing the base, I groaned, going down to my knees first to lap at her.

Her thighs were around my head, clutching me tightly, and I probed at her, my fingers slowly playing with her soft flesh, my beard rough against her inner thighs.

I laughed with her, blowing hot air over her pussy, nibbling, sucking, playing with her clit. And when she shouted my name, her pussy clamping around my fingers, I slid my digits out, licked them clean as she looked at me, her eyes dark, her mouth parted, and then I slid into her.

We didn't need any words, because there weren't any for this.

Instead, her wet heat enveloped me, and my body shook, the base of my spine tingling at first contact. With another inch, I was fully seated, my body rocking against hers. She wrapped her legs around my waist, and I slid one hand around to the back of her head, tilting her so I could devour more of her, my other hand digging into her thigh. I was careful never to squeeze too hard, to hurt her in any way. She was precious to me. She was everything.

How the hell had this happened? How had I fallen so quickly?

Regardless, I loved it, and I thought I might love her.

I kept moving, sharing breaths with her, arching and aching as my cock pulsed deep inside her.

When I slid my hand down her thigh and in between us, brushing along her clit, she broke apart, her cunt wet and tight around my dick. I fell into her, coming hard, filling the condom as I roared her name in my head, but my lips were on hers, so only a breath of passion escaped.

And then we were shaking, still naked in my kitchen, laughing at the absurdity of it all.

Because this wasn't the man I had once been. She wasn't the woman she had been before either. But this was us, and while I knew the ramifications of what had happened earlier would likely come back to haunt me—because they always did—and I knew her ex probably wasn't done with her, right then, I could pretend. I could just be, and that was perfectly fine with me.

Because I had been missing this for far too long.

As her hands stroked me, laughter in her eyes, and heat renewing in her skin, I knew that no matter what, we would have each other when the dam broke and reality invaded.

We would have each other.

Chapter 13

Hazel

I RUBBED MY TEMPLES, TOOK OFF MY READING glasses because they were impeding my rubbing, and then went back to it. I was usually better at focusing and not getting headaches when it came to grading, but I hadn't slept the night before, and that was my fault. Well, mine and Cross's. But I couldn't blame him for that, could I? I was the one who'd slept over. Actually *slept over* at his house, on a school night. I'd had to rush home this morning to make sure I could get ready and dressed on time.

I had barely made it in before my first class, and I

knew that if my friends could see me now, they would think that I looked like a cat in cream.

Or maybe a cat with a canary in its mouth.

I wasn't good at that idiom. I was far better at math. Or so I told myself as I looked down at my grading.

Dustin's homework was in front of me. As I went through it, I nodded along at the progress I saw.

He was trying so hard, but there were still a few parts he wasn't getting. I held up my notebook and took a few notes to try a couple of other pathways for him during our next meeting. He understood far more than he had before, but something wasn't clicking yet. I was going to figure out how to fix that.

Because he was a brilliant kid with a ton of potential. And since I hated the word *potential* because all it did was have negative connotations for the other side of the coin, I would never tell him that. But I was going to show him that he could do this. He could figure this out, and we would find a way to make that happen for him. Dustin had gotten a better grade on the most recent exam than he had on the first one. I could already see the improvement. I needed to stop being so hypercritical of my grading and teaching and just breathe through this.

Dustin would get it. It would take a little time and some patience, but he'd do it. I wasn't very patient in wanting to see my students succeed, though.

I found my reading glasses again, sipped at my now-cooling tea, and went back to grading.

I was nearing my lunch break and knew I should probably leave my desk since I had a headache, so I locked everything away and headed to the other side of the building where I knew I could pick up a sandwich since I hadn't brought a salad or anything else with me today. After all, I'd been a bit preoccupied this morning. And a little late. All because of a certain man, one with very nice looks and an even nicer cock. Not that I was going to think about that right now. I could already feel the color in my cheeks, but I didn't let that bother me.

After all, I wasn't going to be that woman. The one who always thought about the guy she was dating and pretended that everything was fine.

Because we weren't dating. We were past dating. We were in a *relationship*.

Somehow, an accidental blind date had turned into an actual relationship. And I still wasn't a hundred percent sure how that had happened.

But I was fine. I would figure this out. I always did.

I ordered a small sandwich from the café with an iced tea, my water already in my bag, and then took a seat in the corner so I could eat it in peace—surrounded by people but not actually having to communicate.

That was the good thing about the mathematicians in

my department—they knew when to socialize, and when somebody just wanted to sit in a corner surrounded by people but still alone.

I opened my sandwich and started eating, enjoying my lunch and trying to let my brain emerge from its fog.

Of course, my phone took that moment to start buzzing.

I looked down at the group chat and smiled.

All of the girls were working today, but it seemed we had decided to take our lunch break together. Or at least, a text break together.

Paris: *Don't you find it odd that Hazel still hasn't told us much about what she and Cross are doing?*

Myra: *I know, right? I mean, they've been on how many dates together now? And we know she's slept with him at least five times.*

My eyes widened, and I held back a laugh, mostly because I was in public, and no one needed to ask me what this conversation was about.

Dakota: *Hey now, be nice. When it's our turn, don't we deserve a little bit of privacy?*

I always knew I liked Dakota. She understood me.

Dakota: *I changed my mind. I want to know all the details. Tell me. I'm living vicariously through you here.*

Dakota *wasn't* my favorite person.

As the girls continued to text, each one adding more

emojis and exclamation points, I scrolled down and began typing.

Me: *I'm working here, ladies. Isn't this a nighttime conversation?*

Paris: *Aha. You're saying you only do it in at night?*

I put my hand over my mouth, holding back a laugh.

Myra: *You know, maybe Cross only likes it with the lights off.*

Dakota: *And, gasp, missionary.*

I closed my eyes, trying not to laugh, but I knew it was a lost cause.

I snorted, grateful that no one was paying attention to me because they all had their eyes on their own phones, and went back to typing.

Me: *You all are horrible.*

Paris: *But not as horrible as Cross. I mean, if it's awful, you need to tell us.*

Me: How exactly is that any of your business?

Paris: *It's our business because we love you. And we're all bereft. Tell us.*

Myra: *Please? Please? Please?*

Dakota: *Everyone else is begging, so I'm just going to order it. Tell us. We want to know all the details. And since we can't see you, we can't actually ask you to show us the* *distance between your palms to talk about specific attributes.*

Paris: *Just tell us in terms of eggplant emojis.*

This time, I full out laughed, and a few people looked at me. I just waved and pointed at my phone, rolling my eyes.

"YouTube video, have it on mute. But still funny," I said, and they seemed to believe me.

I didn't believe myself.

Me: *Please, stop. I'll give you details in person. I'm not writing it down.*

Paris: *Do we need to bring the good wine? You know, so you feel better? Or do we need to bring shots so we feel better about our lack of love life?*

I smiled, looked down at the phone, and typed again.

Me: *I'd bring the shots, ladies.*

Paris: *Bazinga!*

Myra: *Well then, I guess we're going to have to bring the extra shots. I'll bring the liquor, ladies.*

Dakota: *And I'll bring the baked goods because I think I'm going to have to either soak up that liquor or bury myself in carbs. I could do both.*

I laughed again and then set up a time for us to meet.

I loved my girls and the fact that I could feel this

giddy about a guy again. I had no idea what exactly to feel about that, though.

Because everything felt so new and hot and needy.

I still didn't know exactly what I was doing, but I was enjoying myself. And that had to count for something. Didn't it?

I quickly ate my lunch and then went back to work, doing my best to focus on what was in front of me rather than let worry slide through my system.

Because I had been on this path before, hadn't I? I had felt this happiness before, or at least a version of it.

Things with Cross were far different than they had ever been with Thomas.

But I had married Thomas. I had said my vows to him and promised the future.

And when he hurt me, when he degraded me, I left.

But I hadn't left in time.

And now, he was out, still far away according to the detectives, but what if I was wrong?

What if I was trusting when I shouldn't?

I let that thought simmer. It worried me more than it should, and by the end of the workday, I was a mess. I packed up and headed home, but I didn't text Cross.

I should. I should have seen how he was doing, but I knew he was working and focusing on what to do about Chris.

I didn't text him. I didn't call him.

Instead, I did my regular routine of going home and making sure I was safe, and then I sat on the couch and looked at my phone, wondering if this happiness was just a fluke. After all, it had been once before.

What if it was again?

Chapter 14

CROSS

I STOOD IN MY HOME WORKSHOP, RUNNING MY HANDS through my hair as I tried to figure out what I was going to do next. I had a few projects on my plate. I knew that I would get to them; I always did. I wasn't one of those artists who had to be in the moment at any particular time so I could focus solely on that project. No, I only took the work I wanted to do, and figured out what I needed creatively to start them.

Those projects would come, and I would be ready for them, but for now, I needed to clear my head so I could focus on what I needed to do and then finish up these papers with my lawyer.

I was finally dissolving the partnership, and most likely suing Chris if things didn't get worked out beforehand.

I wasn't going to talk to him again, hence why I was working here, with my lawyer doing most of the work for me so all I had to do was focus on making more money outside of what Chris could steal from me.

I still couldn't believe that he had forged so many fucking documents. But I should, shouldn't I?

After all, that was the whole reason I was leaving the partnership to begin with. Because I didn't trust him. I never should have.

I had lots going on in my head, but it wasn't just Chris on my mind. I was wondering why the hell Hazel hadn't texted me yet.

Usually, we texted throughout the day, but I always let her text me first because her schedule was such that she would likely be surrounded by people. I didn't want to bother her.

So now, I waited. And I seriously hated waiting.

Hell. I'd become a teenage boy, dealing with texting. But I couldn't help myself.

I picked up my phone and looked at the time. She would be out of work by now. Would likely be home. And she hadn't contacted me. Why was I so worried about this?

Things were going fucking fantastic between us. I shouldn't stress out just because everything else in my life was up in the air. Go ahead with Hazel? We were still processing things, but it was good. I wasn't going to fuck it up.

So why did I feel like that was the only thing I was doing these days?

I sighed, glanced around my empty workshop, then picked up my phone.

Me: *Good day at work?*

Good one, Cross.

Jesus. It was like I'd forgotten how to speak to another person—text or not. If she needed space, I should give it to her. This whole relationship thing was new to her, just like it was to me. I hadn't been in a serious relationship because I hadn't found the right person. I thought Hazel might be that person, and it should worry me that I thought that, but it didn't.

No, I wanted more. Maybe that was why I was so nervous.

Hazel: *Sorry, been busy all day. How are you?*

Not many words. Somehow, I felt like I was annoying her.

This whole thing with Chris had me rethinking everything I was doing. What the hell? I was terrible at dating. I had told her multiple times that I was good at other things. Like communicating with fucking people.

Why was I messing up like this?

Me: *Just wanted to see how you were doing since I knew you were working today. I'm at home thinking about what project to start next.*

I looked down at the phone, wondering if I should say anything else. I had no idea what she wanted me to say.

Me: *I missed you.*

There was such a long pause, that I was afraid that I had said the wrong thing, that I'd said too much.

I didn't feel like I was baring my soul. How could I be when I didn't know what she wanted from me?

I felt like I was messing up once again. I didn't even know what I wanted or what she needed.

She had so much emotional baggage. The fact that I was the first person after her ex that she'd been with was a lot.

I didn't want to rush her, but I needed to work through my feelings, too, something I wasn't good at. Something I didn't even like to talk about.

I needed to figure this out. I also needed to give her time.

I just didn't want to wait anymore.

What did that say about me?

Hazel: *I missed you too. The girls were asking about you today.*

That put a smile on my face, and I picked up my phone.

Me: *Yeah?*

Hazel: *There were eggplant emojis involved.*

I barked out a laugh and shook my head.

Me: *How many did you give me?*

Hazel: *Never mind, but don't worry, I'm thinking about exactly what I'm going to tell them in person.*

I laughed again.

Me: *I've heard my sister and the others talk. I know that you ladies like to divulge way more than I'm comfortable with. Just give me a heads up if you're going into too much detail. Because when I finally meet your friends, I don't want to blush like a schoolboy.*

Hazel: *I'm sure it'll all be complimentary. Maybe. We'll see.*

Me: *I sure hope so. I remember exactly what we did last night.*

Hazel: *So do I. Hence why I was a complete mess today at work. I should probably plan better if we're ever going to do that again on a school night.*

If ever? I asked myself. It sure as hell would happen again if I had any say in it.

Me: *Maybe you should just leave clothes at my house.*

Where the hell had that come from? We'd only been together for a little over a month at this point. Almost two if I did the math. Was that enough time for this? I was so new to all of this, even though I wasn't in college or anything anymore. But I'd never been in a situation where I wanted someone's clothes at my house.

She was silent long enough that I was afraid I'd said the wrong thing. Hell, maybe I had.

I had no idea what the fuck I was doing.

Hazel: *Maybe. And I'm not just saying that because I want to change the subject. I just don't know if texting is the best way to talk about that. Like we've both said before, we kinda suck at this.*

Me: *Yeah. I just asked you to leave stuff at my house in a fucking text message.*

Hazel: *And I thought it would be nice if you had a toothbrush over here, and I was going to buy you one because I know you had to use your finger last time because sharing toothbrushes is weird.*

I grinned.

Me: *Considering where we put our mouths with each other, it shouldn't be weird. But you're right, maybe I will leave a toothbrush there.*

Hazel: *Or maybe I'll just get you one.*

I grinned, wondering what I had done in a past life to deserve her.

I didn't know, but I hoped I was doing the right thing now.

I hoped that I wasn't stressing her out. Or making things worse.

Because I was still trying to figure out what I wanted when it came to Hazel, and I knew she had way more baggage than even I did.

Considering that I had a huge family and a coworker who was stealing from me and acting sketchy as fuck, that was saying something.

My fingers moved before I even really knew what was happening.

Me: *When am I going to see you again?*

Hazel: *I think we planned dinner tomorrow, didn't we?*

I cursed.

Me: *I forgot. But yes, dinner tomorrow.*

Hazel: *Thanks for taking your time with me, Cross. I know I seem hot and cold at times, but that's because I'm trying to figure this out.*

I picked up my phone and dialed her number.

"Hey," I said as she answered.

"Hey."

"I was tired of texting. My fingers are too big for this fucking phone."

"I would make a penis joke or ask what exactly you can do with your fingers, but I think we know exactly what you're good at."

I smirked.

"You know. But before you sputter or I say something moronic, just know that I like what we're doing. I know we're both trying to figure this out, but I'm trying to be more open. I'm trying to figure out what I want to say. I'm just not good with words."

"I think you're better than you think you are."

"Oh?" I asked.

"Yes. And thanks for giving me time. I wasn't ready for this, even though I said I was going into dating with that pact and all. I'm just not sure I was ready for you."

We were both silent for a moment, stunned by her honesty. I swallowed hard.

"The Bradys are hard to be ready for."

She laughed, and I was glad that she'd let me off the hook with that remark. Because I didn't know what I wanted, not when my professional life was up in the air.

My family was steady, but work wasn't.

As for Hazel? Why did I feel like she was the other steady part of my life? I barely knew her. We were just figuring out who we were as a couple.

But I felt like we could be something more, and this feeling within me, this gut-churning, scary, palms-going-clammy feeling had to be something.

Did I love her?

I had never loved a woman before. Never said the words, other than to my family.

But as I heard her voice and her laugh as we talked about her day and then mine and just tried to keep ourselves rooted in whatever steadiness we could, I wondered if I loved her.

And then I wondered what that would mean for tomorrow, and the next day, and the next.

Chapter 15

HAZEL

PARIS: *YOU STILL HAVEN'T TALKED ABOUT HIS eggplant. We're going to need the details.*

I crossed my eyes as I looked down at my phone, shaking my head.

It was my day off, and I was meeting Cross later for a date. We might be discussing his eggplant at that point. But I had no plans to talk about it with my friends. Oh, I had joked that I was going to draw it in dramatic detail. But nobody needed to know exactly what I had with Cross beyond my current feelings. Not that I could talk about those. Because I needed to work through them first, and that was the hard part. Figuring out exactly what I wanted and how I could be safe emotionally and physically, then making that happen.

It wasn't going to be easy, not when every time I felt like I could get close to Cross, thoughts of Thomas came back.

That wasn't fair to Cross, and we both knew it. However, I knew he was giving me leeway for that.

But I was here. I was whole enough. I had to be.

Thomas wasn't part of this. He wasn't even near me. He wasn't going to come after me.

He couldn't.

I was safe.

And if I kept telling myself that, I wouldn't live in fear like I did. I might let myself trust Cross and my friends, but I couldn't trust anyone else.

My hand gripped the knife in my hand as I looked down at the lettuce I was cutting, and I slowly forced my fingers to relax, letting the blade go.

Just because I was stressed out and needed to speak with my therapist again, didn't mean I had to bottle my emotions. I was allowed to feel.

I just had to figure out exactly what I was feeling.

I wanted to be with Cross, didn't I? That was the hard part, figuring out exactly what everything meant.

It was if I had some mental block, telling me that I couldn't be with him, even though I should be.

Part of me wanted to be with him. Part of me needed to be with him.

And I didn't know what to do about that yet. He made me happy. He made me smile. He made me really grateful that he had been the one to show up at the bar and not Stavros. Because I knew for a fact that I wouldn't be in this situation if Stavros had been the one to show up. Because there was nobody like Cross.

Right?

I paused and started making my salad, trying to clear my thoughts. Maybe that was the case.

Did I love him? Could I let myself feel that again?

The problem was, I couldn't look back on what I felt for Thomas without remembering the pain of what he'd done. He'd hurt me. Stalked me. Then he'd hurt me again. He was in another state now, out of prison, but still far away, yet part of me still felt like he was right next to me.

And that meant I couldn't entirely trust my feelings.

Yet...yet I'd gone through with the pact for love and finding happiness because I'd wanted to trust those feelings.

So maybe...maybe I *could* love Cross.

And perhaps I could see if he could love me.

I let out a breath and shook my head. There was no use going over and over exactly what I was feeling for Cross. I needed to let myself be. I had to live in the moment.

Something I really wasn't used to.

That wasn't me, the person who could just be. I had to make plans. I had to figure out exactly what I was doing. The fact that I'd even let him sit at my table at all meant that I had already started changing in more ways than I could count.

I wasn't the same woman I had been with Thomas, and I surely wasn't the same person I had become after.

I was a new me, now, one I couldn't quite figure out. But one I needed to decode.

Paris: *Excuse me, you're not answering your texts. Are you playing with his eggplant emoji?*

I laughed out loud and started cleaning off the counter, my salad freshly prepared, before I finally picked up my phone.

Me: *I do believe it's time for us to start on the next phase of this pact because if you're spending so much time discussing a certain eggplant emoji that has nothing to do with you, it's your time.*

Dakota: *I agree with that. It's her time next.*

Myra: *So does that mean you're done? You're happy?*

I paused, trying to decide exactly how to answer that.

Paris: *We can't move on to me unless we know you're settled.*

Me: *Excuse me? I didn't know that was part of the rules. And what do we mean, settled? How settled do I need to be?*

Sweat broke out over my body, and I tried to catch my breath. Settled? I had been married once before and could still remember the heat of his breath on my neck. The way he tugged and pulled at me. The way he made me scream. I didn't want to be married again. Right?

Or was I wrong?

Dakota: *Hey, settled doesn't mean married.*

Myra: *No, settled just means happy. And you haven't told us what you feel. That's all we mean. We don't want to leave you behind as we try to figure out the mess that is Paris's love life.*

I laughed then and shook my head.

Paris: *Excuse me. We are all in the same boat of the what-the-hell of our love lives. You don't need to single me out.*

Myra: *You're next. I'm going to single you out. However, the word* settled *does have connotations that could mean too much for all of us. Perhaps we really do need an explanation.*

I loved when Myra got all technical. She was so

poised and a little elite sometimes, but then she could do shots like nobody's business.

Me: *Let's not discuss the word* settled. *Happy. Does happy work?*

Perhaps.

Me: *Maybe. What does that mean?*

Dakota: *I don't know what Paris means, but from my point of view, I think we should still work on Paris and get started because she's just going to bombard you with eggplant emojis. While we're doing that, we can focus on you, as well. We are smart, funny women who can multitask. Let's do that. We'll multitask in the name of figuring out exactly who the hell we're going to set Paris up with, and how we're going to make sure that you stay happy. Because we want you happy.*

My cheeks warmed, and my stomach clenched, but it wasn't nerves. No, it was the fact that I wasn't alone. I wasn't alone anymore, despite what Thomas had tried for so many years.

I had left him, run from him, and I'd lost everyone from my past. Had almost lost *everything*. Now I had a new family, one that I had chosen.

Cross wasn't part of that. Not yet. But he could be. And that was different for me. Something I was still trying to figure out. He made me happy, and I knew I wasn't alone. I had him. So maybe I just needed to figure out what that meant.

Me: *I'm meeting Cross later tonight for dinner. I'm not going to discuss eggplant emojis with you, but let's just say, there's enough eggplant to go around. But I'm not sharing.*

I laughed out loud at all the emojis the other girls sent, mostly eggplants and peaches and wide-eyed little faces.

My friends were dorks, but then again, so was I. It's why we got along. Because we'd all been hurt in more ways than one, only some of us didn't talk about it as much.

But we were trying. We had made a pact to start dating for a reason. Because we were lonely and needed something more in our lives.

Somehow, even when I wasn't looking, Cross had become that person for me.

Did I love him? I didn't know.

However, I was enjoying the fact that I was free to find out.

My phone buzzed, and Cross's name appeared on the screen.

Cross: *Hey, can you stop by the shop?*

I frowned. I was supposed to meet him at his place because he was going to cook for me. Not at his shop. In fact,

I had never actually been there. He was staying away from it as much as he could these days because he was still trying to make plans for what came next with Chris. I understood that and didn't want to make things more difficult for him. But maybe he wanted to show me his art. I loved watching him work. Even though I'd only really seen it happen at his home studio. I didn't mind dropping by the store.

Me: *What time?*

Cross: *Whenever you can. Earlier, the better. Can't wait to see you. XO.*

I frowned again. *XO?* That didn't sound like him. Or maybe that was just him trying to figure out the next stage of our relationship.

Cross: *Sorry about the XO, I'm trying out a new thing. You know me. Inept.*

That made me laugh, and it sort of made more sense. A little.

Me: *I like XOs. Though I think I like them more in person.*

Cross: *Get here quick, and we can do that.*

I blushed, my whole face heating, and then I smiled.

Me: *Be there soon.*

Cross: *Good. The sooner, the better.*

That was good. That's all he wanted. I didn't know why he wanted me to meet him at Chris Cross, though I didn't want to wait for lunch to see him either. I stuffed my salad back into the fridge, knowing I would eat it later. I didn't want to wait to head over. He wanted me there and this feeling of being wanted had been so foreign before Cross. The fact that he was trying meant everything to me. And while I was attempting to figure out exactly what I wanted to do with my life, maybe he was figuring it out with me, too. That wasn't something I'd truly let myself think about before. But now that I had, I couldn't wait to find out.

I got ready, fixing my makeup and hair, and then put my bag in the car with me. I would be leaving a few things at his house. My stomach clenched at the thought. This was a big step. Not living together, no, neither of us was ready for that yet, but it was us figuring out who we were together. And that was a big thing.

I drove to the other side of the neighborhood and then down the highway a bit to where Cross's shop was located, pulling into the back. I saw another car that I didn't recognize and hoped it wasn't Chris's. I hadn't even thought about that. I hadn't met the man, but I didn't want to find him here. I honestly wouldn't know what to say to him. Maybe Cross was parked in the front, I wasn't a hundred percent sure, but I was sure he was here somewhere. After all, he had just texted me.

I made my way around the building to the front and

knocked, wondering exactly how I was supposed to get in. The door opened, and I took a step back, fear suddenly crawling over my face, my body. The hair on the back of my neck stood on end as I looked at the man in front of me, someone that I didn't recognize. He had wide eyes, dark hair, and an almost soft smile on his face, even as he looked confused for a second.

"Can I help you?" he asked, his voice deep and gruff.

I cleared my throat. "Chris?" I asked, my body shaking. I already had one hand in my purse, ready to use my pepper spray if needed. Not that I wanted to do that on a stranger, especially someone that worked with Cross, but I couldn't be too careful. A scowl covered the man's face, and he shook his head.

"No, I'm Macon. Who are you?" he asked, his voice even gruffer.

Relief spread through me, and I smiled again.

I knew that name. *Macon.* I had never heard of another person with that name, so this had to be Cross's brother.

"I'm Hazel. Sorry, I haven't met you before, so I didn't know who you were."

Surprise covered Macon's features, and he smiled at me then, his face brightening.

"Hello there. Come on in. I'm just here to pick up something for Cross."

I frowned and halted. "What do you mean?" I asked as the door closed behind me.

"Huh?"

"What do you mean you're here to pick up something for Cross? He texted me and told me to meet him here."

Macon shook his head. "That doesn't make sense. I was just on the phone with him. He said that he needed me to pick up something since he was at the house cooking for you. I wondered why you were here."

Fear crawled over me, and I took a step back towards the door.

"Macon, I really think we need to go."

"No, I really think you should stay," a voice said from the darkness as a shadow came forward, and then another. Macon was in front of me in a second, and then I had my hands up, pepper spray in one, my other hand on Macon's back, trying to figure out what the hell was going on.

"You always were stupid," a familiar voice said. I froze, my whole body shaking. But before I even had time to react, before I had time to think, I heard a shot, and then a scream, and then Macon was on top of me.

And I could scent the blood in the air.

Chapter 16

CROSS

I TURNED DOWN THE WARMER ON THE MEAL I'D MADE and frowned. Hazel hadn't called me or texted me back since I'd last talked to her that morning when I made sure that we were still on for dinner. Macon hadn't stopped by with the piece of equipment I needed after I'd asked him to stop by and pick it up for me either. I had been focused on getting everything ready for my lawyer and then making dinner for Hazel, and I had forgotten something that I needed to complete my project over the weekend. I had been on the phone with Macon when I mentioned it, and he had offered to stop by and pick it up.

And yet neither of them was calling or texting me back. I was worried, but I was trying not to be. I figured I was on the way to becoming paranoid at this point. Still, why the fuck weren't they answering?

I ran my hands through my hair and over my beard and then started pacing around the kitchen, calling Hazel's number one more time.

It rang and rang before the voicemail picked up.

"This is Hazel. Please leave a message after the beep. Thanks."

"Babe, it's me. Pick up. Please. You're starting to worry me."

I hung up. I even called Macon, but he didn't answer either.

I left a message for him and then called Prior.

"Hey, has Macon called you today?" I asked.

"No, I haven't talked to him. What's up?"

"I can't get ahold of him. Or Hazel, for that matter. Something's wrong, I know it."

"I'll call Nate. You call Arden."

"Thanks. But...hell. There has to be something wrong."

"Macon is probably just in the zone, didn't hear his phone. And your girl is probably on her way and can't pick up her cell. Everything's fine. It's not going to be anything bad."

"Do you really believe that?" I said, my hands shaking.

"Maybe, but we're going to pretend like everything is fucking fine. Let's get on that."

I hung up and called Arden.

"I haven't talked with her or Macon, I'm sorry. Let me call Liam and the others. I think I might have one of the girls' numbers, too."

I paused. "You do?" I asked.

"Yes, it's a small world, and we're in a small town. I happen to know people, even if I don't leave the house all that often. Now, let me try and make sure everything's fine."

I didn't question her further, though I had a feeling that Arden was keeping a secret.

I hung up after saying goodbye. When my phone rang again, I answered quickly, not recognizing the number.

"Hazel? Macon?"

"No, it's Frank from across the street. From Chris Cross. You better get over here, Cross. Looks like somebody torched your place."

My body went cold, and bile filled my throat.

"What?"

"Your place. It's on fire. You'd better get here quick."

"Thanks, Frank." My hands shook, and I wanted to throw up. Macon. Macon was there. That's why he wasn't answering his phone. Was Hazel there, too? But why would she be? There was no reason for her to be at the shop. Unless...unless...I didn't fucking know. I grabbed my keys, my hands shaking, and got in my car. I practically sped to Chris Cross. I was thankful that no cops pulled me over, because I was going over the speed limit more than I should have been. I might have run a red light, too. Honestly, I didn't care.

I got there and almost fell to my knees.

The whole place was on fire, flames licking at the sky. I just looked around, wondering what the hell I was going to do. We had insurance, but who the fuck cared about that right now?

"Macon!"

I coughed as I move forward, the heat searing my skin as I looked around.

"Macon!"

"Cops are on their way, son," Frank said, and I turned to see a group of people.

"Did you see my brother? He might have been here."

Frank's eyes turned somber, and he shook his head.

"I'll help you look, son. I'll help you look."

I moved forward. I knew this was stupid, but I had to find my brother. I had to find Macon.

I went around to the back parking lot, and my knees shook because I recognized the car parked there.

Hazel. Hazel was here, too.

Oh my God.

I kept going to the back door—it didn't seem the flames had reached there yet—but I couldn't open it, I couldn't get closer. Then I saw the pile of clothes and the lump on the other side of the porch. I leapt over it, fell to my knees, and turned over my brother's body.

Blood covered his chest, and my whole body shook. I put my hands over the wound, blood seeping through my fingers.

But his blood was still pumping, which meant, he was alive.

"Macon? Macon."

"Hazel," Macon ground out.

"What?" My hands shook as I put pressure on my brother's chest. "Where's Hazel, Macon? What happened? Who did this?"

"They took her. They took Hazel. Find her."

And then Frank was there, on his knees next to me, his hands over mine.

"They took your girl? Is that what I heard?" Frank said.

"Where?" I asked Macon, my hands trembling under Frank's.

Macon pointed weakly. "Trees. I'll be fine. Find her."

I couldn't choose. Tears stung my eyes. I didn't want

to leave my baby brother. There was blood on my hands, swaths of red everywhere, and he was coughing.

And someone had taken Hazel.

I didn't know what to do.

"I'm good," Macon said and smiled, an expression that reached his eyes like it always did. I was going to throw up.

"I'll be right back," I whispered, then leaned down and kissed my brother on the cheek because he wasn't going to die. This wouldn't be the last time I saw him.

Macon's hand slid up, his whole arm shaking as he touched my cheek.

"Find her. I'm fine."

And then Frank pushed me out of the way and gave me a tight nod.

"Find your girl. I've got this. Cops are almost here."

Frank had been saying that over and over, and I wanted to believe him. I wanted to believe both of them. So I got to my feet, staggering a little, and looked down at my little brother. Then, I turned away.

Because I had to find Hazel.

No matter what.

Chapter 17

HAZEL

THE GUNSHOT STILL RANG IN MY EARS, AND MY hands shook. This couldn't be happening. This could not be happening.

As I looked above me at Macon's pale face, pain evident in his eyes, I knew it was. And there was no going back. That was a shot. Someone had shot at us.

No, not someone. I knew exactly who it was. And I also knew there was no going back. There had never been any going back.

Macon rolled off me but still kept me behind him, my hands on his chest as I tried to stop the bleeding. Everything was moving so fast, and there was screaming in my head, but not aloud. I couldn't speak, couldn't do anything.

No amount of pepper spray or security cameras were going to save me now.

Everything I'd thought I had done to protect myself had been for nothing.

Thomas was here.

And he wasn't alone.

Somehow, he had lured me here. Macon had already been here, and now he was bleeding on me. I was covered in his blood.

I couldn't breathe.

Why couldn't I breathe?

"Run," Macon whispered, his voice hoarse.

But there was no running. I never really had a chance to run.

It had all been a lie. The idea that I could hide and have a life of my own. None of that was true.

There was no going back.

This was my life now, just like it had always been.

"Help me get her up."

I looked up at the sound of Thomas's voice as another man came forward, his face pale, and his hands shaking.

"I didn't know we were going to shoot him. Holy fuck. I just wanted my money. You came to me. You said you knew her. That she took from you. That all I needed to do was get her. That I would get my money from Cross, and that everything would be fine and I could get away. What the fuck? Why are we shooting people? Oh my God. That's Macon. That's Cross's fucking brother."

This was Chris. It had to be.

All of this was for money? No, for Chris maybe. But Thomas never wanted money. He just wanted me.

But this wasn't my blood on my hands. It was Macon's.

Cross's brother was going to die, and I couldn't save him.

His life's blood slid through my fingers. I tried to help him, but then I felt hands on me, and then I was screaming aloud, yelling and kicking.

"You bitch." I felt a slap to my face. My jaw hurt, and I crossed my eyes, trying to see. Chris glared at me, his arm back as if to hit me again.

"Don't hurt her too badly," Thomas said, his voice sly and dark. "That's my job."

I moved faster, trying to get away, but Chris's grip on my shoulders tightened.

"Stop it. Stop fighting. You're just going to make it harder for yourself."

I fought even harder.

I expected the second slap, and then felt another as

Chris hit me again and again, his ring slicing my skin near my hairline.

Blood ran down my face, but I didn't care. I had to get out of here.

There was no going back. I had to move.

"I didn't sign up for this. I didn't know we were going to do any of this," Chris complained.

"You want your money, you'll finish what we started. It's as easy as that. You shouldn't have let me into your little building last week if you were so scared. I followed my *wife* and found out she was with that sad excuse for a man. Lucky for me, his name is so unusual, and I could find this place. And you."

Thomas smiled then, and my skin crawled. I hated that smile. He'd smiled like that before he'd hit me. Before he stalked me when I tried to run away. He'd smiled at me like that the last time before he'd been put away, locked up, behind bars.

But now he was here. Out of jail. And *here*.

What was I going to do? I had to do something.

Macon.

Macon was hurt.

I needed to help him.

I needed help.

"You came to *me*, telling me that you had a way for me to get out of my agreement with Cross. That I wouldn't get in trouble for skimming my invoices a bit." Chris paused, confused. "How did you know that anyway?"

"I listened. How the hell do you think I knew? You never shut up about it. You were an opportunity, Christopher. A good one. And if you don't start moving, you'll be a dead one."

"Don't fucking threaten me!"

Thomas held up his hands, that smile back on his face. "You're right. We're...partners. I shouldn't threaten. My apologies. However, we really must get a move on if we're going to get out of here before anyone else arrives. For all we know, Cross will show up and perhaps the authorities."

I was stilled pinned to the ground, listening to the two, trying to catch up. So that's how Thomas knew Chris? By *chance*? Opportunity?

And now Macon was dying, and I didn't know how I was going to get out of this.

"Fuck. What about Macon?"

Thomas shrugged as I continued thrashing. I felt dizzy, blood pooled in my mouth.

There was blood on my hands too, but not my blood. No, it was Macon's. Macon's.

"I don't care what you do with him. Leave him here, do whatever. You know what you have to do to the building when we're done anyway. It's not really my problem from this point on. You wanted your money, we'll get to that. But I need her. And that was the promise."

I screamed, but then Chris's hands were on my mouth, stifling the sound. I could barely breathe. I fought, but he hit me again. I couldn't do much. Everything hurt, but still I kicked and dug my heels into the carpet as I tried to get out. But he was so much bigger than I was, and I couldn't do anything.

He pinned my arms over my head and dragged me. I realized that no amount of kicking or twisting was going to work.

There was nothing I could do, but still, I tried.

"Stop fucking screaming," Thomas said, his hand right in front of my face.

If you don't fucking stop, I'll kill him right here. He still has a chance. He's still breathing. I don't think the bullet punctured a lung. But what do I know? I only know how to hurt you. I don't really know how to heal you, isn't that right? You're the one who put me in jail. So really, this is all your fault."

I listened to Thomas's diatribe, my whole body freezing.

"That's a good girl." He tapped my chin with the gun, the end still warm, the heat of it singeing my skin.

"Be a good girl, and maybe he can live. You fight Chris one more time, and I'll shoot your little friend in the head. You fucking him like you're fucking his brother? Because I'm pretty sure you were always a whore. I tried to clean you up, but that was never good enough, was it?"

I didn't say anything. I couldn't. I couldn't let Macon die. I couldn't let Cross's brother die.

"See? You've already learned your place. Be a good girl, and you won't hurt too much more. But you know I love your screaming. When we're in a better place, you can scream all you want. You're going to need to, you fucking bitch."

Thomas hit me, this time with the gun in his hand, and everything went dark.

I opened my eyes again as he dragged me out into the trees behind the building. I could just see a shadow on the porch behind Chris Cross.

Macon.

He was crawling towards us. He was trying, doing so much, and yet it wasn't enough. He was going to die trying to help me. He was going to die trying to save himself. And there was nothing I could do.

More blood pooled in my mouth, and I spit it out, trying to focus, trying to do something. Anything. All those self-defense classes, and yet none of it helped against a gun.

I moved again, trying to twist my body. Someone

kicked me in the side, I didn't know who it was, Thomas or Chris, but I knew I'd have a footprint on my flesh.

Honestly, it didn't matter who it was. It could be either one. This would be how it ended.

They dragged me through the trees, the rocks digging into my legs and back. I had cuts and abrasions forming all over my body, yet I didn't feel it. Only the pain in my head and arms from where they dragged me.

They pulled me toward a wood cabin I hadn't realized was there, and I let out a breath, trying to focus. There had to be something I could do, some way out of this. Only I didn't think so.

"She won't stop fucking moving," Chris grumbled as he tossed me onto the floor. The grain of the wood dug into my cheek as my head slammed down. I swore my teeth ratted, and I instinctively moved my hands to try and calm the throbbing in my face.

"What did I say, pet?" Thomas asked, his voice low and steady.

Too steady for a man with no soul.

"I'll go back and kill him if you don't stop moving."

He paused.

"In fact, Chris, I have one last thing for you to do. It'll help cover up any of your misdeeds."

"What?

"There's gasoline on the side of the building. You know what to do."

I froze, my whole body shaking.

"And Macon?" Chris asked, his throat working hard as he swallowed.

"Kill him. I don't care. Just take care of the building. Then get back to me. If you want the money."

Chris looked frozen for a second, as if he didn't know what to do, but then he was off. Fear crawled over me, its silky fist smooth around my throat, my heart, everything.

"That's a good girl," Thomas said, his hand around my throat.

I didn't move because I wasn't sure what they were going to do with Macon—or what they would do with me.

"I waited so long for you, Hazel. Why did you leave me? You should've stayed with me. You tried to get away. I found you. Then you sent me to jail. Why?"

I opened my mouth to speak, but he slapped me again. Tears stung my eyes.

"No. This isn't the time for you to speak. We're done with that." He turned away from me before facing me once more.

"You're going to listen. *You put me in jail.* How could you do that to me? I was everything to you. I was yours. You took my gifts for granted and spat in my face. You were always a whore, I knew that going in. But I took care of you. I always cherished you. But instead of accepting my benevolence, you threw it in my face."

He started to pace, and I looked around the old cabin, trying to figure out exactly how I could get out. But I couldn't.

There was nothing I could do. Maybe if I moved my hand a little bit towards the side, I could figure a way out of these bindings he'd just put me in.

But I had to be careful because he was watching me. Like always, he was watching me.

"I did good. For you. I stayed away just long enough for you to miss me. But then you were with him. That fucking asshole. You like beards and being a whore? I didn't realize that about you. You fucking whore."

He hit me again, and tears slid down my cheeks, my entire body racked with pain.

"Look what you made me do. You're making me hurt you because you just don't understand what I need. You used to. But now, you don't."

He let out a breath, then continued. "I married you because you were mine. Our families were always associated, and your parents gave you to me. You were a gift. My perfect gift, and then you threw me away."

"That's not what happened," I said, my voice hoarse. "Thomas. You have to stop. Please. Don't take this any further."

"I said, shut up!"

He slapped me again, the sting warm against my cooling flesh.

"I've always watched you. I've always known where you are. No matter how safe you thought you were online, you were never safe enough. I texted you. Told you I saw you. Because I always see you, pet. But you never returned my texts. And when I got out, you never visited. When I got past my lazy parole officer and drove all the way here to find you, you weren't waiting. You had your little security system at your home like you used to for me in our game, but I still got through. I had ways. I was always good at that. You remember. I had money, yes, but I am also brilliant. You know that. You know that I learned computer hacking and other games for us to play."

Games? He thought my fear was a game.

I'd never been so wrong in my life. I'd never screwed up as badly as I had when I fell for Thomas. And now I was paying the price.

And Macon was, too.

"I came here for *you*. For *us*. And where did I find you? Fucking another man in our bed!"

I'd thrown away the bed I'd shared with him, but I didn't say that. It didn't matter. He was in his own world now, and I was only a pawn.

"You were supposed to be my perfect wife. It's going

to take me way too long to teach you the ways of how I need you to be now. Why do you have to be so difficult?"

I didn't open my mouth to speak this time. He didn't expect an answer.

"All I wanted was you, and you lied. You put me in jail. I suffered because of you. Now, you're going to suffer through every little thing that I was forced to endure inside that jail cell. That prison cell," he amended, his voice shrill.

"I hate you, but yet, I love you. You're going to learn to love me. And you're going to forget that bearded asshole. You're going to forget him, and you're never going to want him again. I was always the one for you. You let him fuck you, I'll just fuck you harder. You let him touch you, I'll scrape every inch of skin off your body."

Fear slammed into me, and my whole body shook, my stomach revolting, bile filling my mouth.

"I see you get it." A sick grin twisted his lips.

"You were always mine, yet you dared to give yourself to another. Now, you'll pay the price."

Chris interrupted from the doorway. "First, though, I need my money. Let's get that business done. I didn't want this. Not this blood and shit. But we're here, and I need my money from Cross's accounts. From *my* accounts." My head turned to him at the same time Thomas's did. My eyes widened, and I wondered what the hell he was doing. Cross had said that Chris had stolen from him, but this?

There was blood on his hands, and I looked down at them, tears falling freely from my eyes. He smelled like smoke and gasoline.

And Macon wasn't with him.

Cross's brother was dead, all because of me. All of this was because of me.

"I've got your payment right here."

There was another shot, and Chris's gaze went from surprised to glassy in an instant as he fell to his knees, part of his head blown off, blood and brain matter coating the wall behind him.

I opened my mouth and screamed.

Chapter 18

CROSS

THE SOUND OF THE GUNSHOT RICOCHETED IN MY ears, and I froze for a second. Fuck. No. It couldn't be her. She had to be alive. This wasn't fucking happening.

I kept going, doing my best to head to where I had heard the shot. There were drag marks in the ground. Was it her? It had to be. The tracks looked too fresh. I wasn't an actual tracker, I had never been hunting, but I could follow these. They were so prevalent that I couldn't *not* follow them.

I knew the cops and others were following me, or at least they would be soon. I was stupid for coming out on my own, but I couldn't just leave her here. I had no weapon, I had nothing, but I had myself.

I couldn't let her be alone. Not after everything that had happened to her.

I kept going and turned a corner, following the path the tracks had made. I stumbled into a tree as I looked in front of me. I knew this area. Had walked back here before. The lights of the cabin in front of me were on, but only by a couple lanterns. She had to be in there. And I knew she wasn't alone.

I dropped to my knees, just in case someone was looking out the window, and finally got a good look at the door.

It was open, light shining like a beacon in the dark. My heart stopped.

There was a body there, feet out the door, blood pooling. I knew those shoes.

Jesus Christ, it was Chris.

And Chris wasn't moving.

And then I heard a man screaming, and a woman whimpering, and I knew who that was.

It was Hazel, my Hazel.

Jesus Christ.

There was no more time to think or plan because they were shouting again. Then I heard another gunshot and immediately got to my feet.

I didn't know what I was doing, and I knew I would likely get myself killed, but I had to save her. I had to do something. I wasn't some tragic hero in a thriller movie, who had a weapon and knew what the fuck I was doing.

All I had was myself, and what little time we had left.

I ran and jumped over Chris's body, ignoring the brains and the blood and whatever the fuck else was around him, and slammed into the man looming over Hazel.

I threw myself on top of the man who had to be Thomas—who else would it be?—even though I had no idea what he would be doing here or why. Thankfully, the shadows from the window gave me a sense of where everybody was positioned so I could hit my mark.

Hazel screamed, and I saw her thrashing on the floor, moving her hands as if she were trying to break free of restraints.

I landed on top of the other man, and the gun fell to the floor, sliding across the wood planks.

"You fucking bastard," the other man growled beneath me and punched out. I didn't have time to move off him quickly enough, so the fist landed on my jaw. But I didn't move, I hit him back, and then again.

We rolled on the floor, the man larger than me, apparently having used the weights at the prison long enough to bulk up.

But maybe this wasn't even Thomas.

It didn't matter who he was.

This man had shot my brother, had killed Chris, and had Hazel.

Fuck this shit.

"Cross, watch out!" I ducked the other man's fist at Hazel's warning, and then punched him again, this time hard enough that the guy's eyes rolled back, and he passed out, his whole body going lax.

I staggered to my feet, leaving him where he fell, and ran towards Hazel.

"Baby, oh my God."

"Quick, help me get out of these, I'm almost out of the restraints, but they're digging into my right wrist, and I can't get free."

She was rambling, not making much sense. I needed to run my hands over her and catalog every single cut and bruise. There were so many. She was covered in blood, her face bruised, and I knew there were probably more injuries I couldn't see.

That fucker.

"Let's get you out of here. The cops are on their way."

"Good. Macon. I'm so sorry, Cross. Thomas. It was Thomas. My ex. He shot Macon."

I froze, my hands shaking. Her ex? It *was* her ex. Fucking hell. My mind went in a million different directions and I didn't know what to say, what to think, so I didn't. She was safe—or would be. And my brother *had* to be safe. There was no other option. I pushed all of those thoughts from my brain, however jumbled they were, and finally answered.

"The cops should have him by now. He should be safe," I said.

At least, I hoped so.

I'd left my brother bleeding and to be handled by strangers so I could save Hazel. I never would have forgiven myself if either of them had died.

My hands were shaking as I got her out of the final restraint, and then I lifted her to her feet, both of us moving to get out of there.

Suddenly, there was a noise behind me. I turned, covering Hazel with my body as the shot rang out.

Fire singed my side, and I staggered back, falling to my knees. I felt Hazel's hands on my back as if she were trying to catch me, but I was too heavy for her.

Blood flowed from my side, and I looked down and cursed.

The guy had been faking. Or, I hadn't hit him hard enough.

I looked up as the other man sneered at me, blood covering his chin and forehead from where I had hit him, his arm trembling, and the gun shaking in his hand.

"She's mine," he growled out.

"Never yours," Hazel whispered.

I tried to reach out to her, attempted to tell her that we'd make it out, that we'd be safe, but everything was going dark. I cursed under my breath.

I was losing blood too quickly. I just had to hope like hell that the cops would get here soon.

They had to have followed where I had gone. Followed the sounds. The drag marks left such an easy trail.

Hopefully, Frank could tell them where I had gone. And Macon, too. After all, he had told me.

I couldn't really think right then, though. All I knew was that I needed to make sure Hazel was going to be okay. And my baby brother. And everyone else.

But I couldn't focus.

"Come closer to me, Hazel. Get closer to me, and I won't hurt him again. But you keep touching him, and I'll shoot him right in the fucking head."

"I'm fine, don't listen to him. Save yourself," I whispered.

"So valiant. And yet, she'll still come to me. She always will."

And then Hazel squeezed my shoulder just a bit before she stood on shaky legs. I tried to reach out to her, but my hands slid against her blood-slick ones, and I cursed.

"Don't hurt him," she said, her voice far stronger than I thought possible.

"As long as you're mine, I won't hurt anyone else."

And then she moved forward as the other man held out his arm for her.

I tried to stop her, but I was too weak, the blood loss taking over. When he tugged on her hair, I shouted, and she screamed. Then, everything moved almost too fast to track.

He moved towards her, gun still trained on me, but then she moved, elbowing him in the gut, kicking him in the knee. Thomas shouted.

I got to my feet, ignoring the pain, forgetting about the blood loss, but it was too late.

The gun went off again. I couldn't hear anything, couldn't focus, couldn't breathe. But I still kept moving, kept going.

Because Hazel was there, the gun in her hand, her whole body shaking, and Thomas was on the floor, looking up at her with wide eyes, blood blossoming on his chest.

Carefully, she set the gun on the floor, out of reach of anyone, and I went to her, my knees going weak. I fell at her feet, and she came to me, holding me close. I couldn't say anything.

Because death surrounded us. So much blood, so much horror.

I saw death in her eyes. She didn't say anything, though I didn't know what there was to say.

Finally, when I heard other voices, and the sound of the authorities finally arriving, I just held her close and hoped to hell that we could get through this.

I didn't know how, though. I wasn't sure we could.

And as I looked at her face, I didn't know if she believed we could either.

Chapter 19

Hazel

"That's all for now, Miss Noble. We'll get back with you if we have more questions, but from a personal standpoint, I want to apologize that any of this happened. I'm sorry that you had to go through this."

I looked up into the kind eyes of the detective and nodded, giving him a smile that I knew didn't reach my eyes. It didn't matter. I wasn't feeling much of anything at the moment.

When the detectives left my hospital room, the questions done for now, I looked down at my hands and wondered why they weren't stained with blood.

They should be. After all, I had killed a man. I had been covered with more blood than my own over the course of the evening, and no matter how much antiseptic shower gel slid over my body, it would never be enough to wash it away.

I had Macon's blood on me, perhaps some of Chris's, Cross's, mine, and then Thomas's.

So much blood.

When the cops came, everything moved so quickly, it had taken me a moment to catch up.

Somehow, they had gotten the story of what had happened without arresting me in the process.

I was a little surprised about that. Apparently, Frank, whoever that kind stranger had been, had explained everything to them.

And they had taken me away to heal up, not to jail. They had hurried Cross into surgery. Macon, as well.

Chris was dead, a bullet to the head with his brains splattered against the wall.

And Thomas was now dead, too.

I had pierced his heart with a single bullet, hot, molten steel sliding through his body as it took his soul, his life, and a part of me with it. Not because I loved him, but because I'd been the one to take the shot in the end.

I had killed a man.

And I didn't know what to do about that.

I could remember every single abuse and injury that I had sustained when I was with Thomas the first time.

I couldn't remember every little shove and degrading comment, but I remembered most of them.

That had been a part of my life for so long. Somehow, I had found a way to move on and become a new person.

But then he'd come back, and now here I was, covered in his blood—even though it had been washed away—coated in the blood of so many. Perhaps there was no coming back from this.

How was I supposed to live in a world where I was a murderer? I knew they wouldn't call me that. They would say that I had protected myself and others, that it had been self-defense. I would never see jail time because how could I when it wasn't my fault?

But that was a lie, wasn't it? This *was* all my fault.

If I had stayed away, not gotten involved with Cross, then Thomas wouldn't have become so jealous. Clearly, he had already found me. I should have known that he wouldn't be content to only use texts or his friends to harass me.

He had become jealous and wanted me back in any way he could.

He had found Chris, a tie to Cross. Had somehow convinced him to come to his side. Although, in reality, maybe it hadn't taken too much convincing. Just dollar signs for a man who thought he was already losing every-thing when Cross dissolved the partnership.

But now Chris was dead. There would be no more partnership.

Chris had cloned Cross's phone to lure me to the shop. Had likely known somehow, deep down, what would happen to me, but he hadn't cared.

Still, I didn't want the man to die.

I didn't want death on my hands at all. But now, I was covered in it.

It wasn't just on my soul, it was on every inch of my body, on every ounce of breath I held within me.

Chris had burned the shop to the ground, the gasoline he used only a small accelerant to what was already inside the building. After all they used wood for their work. The place was gone, so much of Cross's livelihood and work gone in an instant.

And if Macon hadn't crawled his way out of the building to try and find me, to attempt to get help, he would probably be dead, too.

But Frank and the others had found him. This mirac-ulous man named Frank, who had kept Macon alive until the paramedics showed up.

Now, Macon was in surgery, the doctors doing their best to repair the bullet wound in his chest.

No one was in the room with me, so I didn't know

how it had all turned out. Didn't know if he was even out of surgery yet. Was Macon out and healthy, or would the Bradys have to say goodbye to their son?

To their brother. Their friend.

The detectives had told me that Cross was in surgery too, another doctor sewing up one of that family. Of everyone in that cabin, I was the only one without a bullet in my body.

It didn't matter that I had bruised ribs, or that I was lucky I hadn't broken my cheekbone or my jaw. It didn't matter that I would have a black eye for a week or that my entire body felt as if I had been pummeled over and over.

It didn't matter that I had bandages around my wrists from where I had pulled against my restraints so hard that the ropes had dug into my skin, leaving bloody gashes behind.

None of that mattered.

Here I was, healthy and whole, but I was a murderer.

Others were dying or dead because of me.

And I had no idea how to change that.

"I'm fine," I said, though I knew it was a lie.

My voice was hoarse, my tongue swollen from when I'd bitten it during the fall.

I would have to get my hair cut because Chris and Thomas had pulled so hard that I had lost clumps, my scalp bloody from it.

All these things spun in my head at the same time, and I couldn't focus.

"What are you thinking about?" Dakota asked, moving toward me.

I raised my chin slightly and tried to act like I was steady.

I didn't even know what the word meant anymore.

"I want to go home," I whispered.

And hide there until I could breathe again. Could think.

"You can do that soon. They're going to let you out since you don't need to be held for observation. But let's talk about it. Or not. Whatever you need, we're here."

I looked at Myra, and I couldn't breathe, I couldn't think.

"I just want to go home," I repeated.

"We're here for you. We love you."

I shook my head.

"He got hurt because of me," I whispered.

"Cross? No," Paris snapped.

"He got hurt because of that asshole," she growled. I flinched at her tone.

Myra and Dakota both gave her admonishing looks, but Paris didn't back down.

"No. You're not going to blame yourself for this. What

happened is not your fault. This is all on Thomas. Not you."

"I know," I lied.

I didn't know if they believed me, but I didn't care. I just wanted to go home. I wanted to be alone. I needed to make sure Cross and Macon were out of surgery, that there would be no ill effects. That they would be able to go home soon and pretend like nothing had happened.

I needed them to be safe.

There was a knock on the door, and Arden stood there, her eyes tired. She didn't look on the verge of breaking down like I was, so I had to hope it meant there was good news.

Dakota and Paris turned on a dime, and both of them moved out of the way for Arden.

But it was Myra that I was looking at, her face pale, her eyes wide. She looked at Arden, and I wondered what had happened. Myra gave a slight shake of her head, and Arden nodded slightly. I knew I had to know what these two were doing. Did they know each other? Had they met before?

I didn't know if it was any of my business, but something was off.

My head hurt too much to focus on it, though, so instead, I raised my chin and tried to pretend that I was fine.

I didn't even know what that meant anymore.

"I said I'm sorry we're meeting like this," Arden said softly. "I wanted to let you know that both Macon and Cross are out of surgery."

My heart shuddered, and I nodded, but I didn't cry. I had a feeling I was done crying.

"That's good news," Dakota said, reaching out with shaking hands to grip Arden's. The other woman clasped my friend's fingers tightly and nodded.

"They're going to be fine. The doctor just came out and told me. My husband's in the waiting room, he wanted to give you some space, but if you need anything, we're all here for you. You're not alone in this, Hazel. I just wanted you to know that. Thank you for both of my brothers' lives. I know it's a bit much, but if you need to talk, we're here."

I nodded, but I didn't really hear any of it. Saving? No, I was the reason they were in this hospital.

And I didn't have them, not really. I didn't have anyone.

I didn't deserve them.

Arden looked between us all and then nodded before walking out, whispering something to Myra on her way by.

Myra gave a tight nod and then closed the door behind Arden.

No one was going to talk about the elephant in the room, about what we had just seen, and that was fine with me.

All I wanted was to go home.

I wanted to be alone.

"Now, let's figure out what to do next," Dakota said.

I shook my head. "Can I just have some space for a minute?" I whispered.

"No, space isn't going to help," Paris said, but Myra shushed her.

"I agree that space isn't going to help, but is that really what you want right now?" Myra asked.

I looked at my friend and wondered what secrets she had, what other things we were all keeping close.

My past had almost gotten two people killed and had led another to getting his head blown off.

"I just need to breathe. Thank you for being here, but I can do this on my own."

Paris opened her mouth to speak again, but Dakota shook her head.

"We'll give you some space for now. Because we love you. But we're not leaving you alone again. And honestly, we're not leaving you alone completely."

"I know," I whispered, my voice wooden.

"We're not staying gone for long," Paris said, glaring at me. But then they all leaned forward. They didn't hug me because I was in pain, but they did run their hands down my arms before leaving me alone.

I lay in my hospital bed for another hour, listening to the nurses come and go. When the doctor said I could leave, that there were three women outside ready to take me home, I didn't hold back a smile. I didn't have anything to smile about, but I did let the warmth slide through me for a bare instant before it iced over.

"Thank you," I whispered.

"You're welcome. We'll talk soon," the doctor said. Then, I was alone again, just like I wanted.

I changed into sweats and a long-sleeved shirt that one of the girls had brought me, and then I slid my feet into my slip-on shoes, wondering where they had taken my other clothes.

I didn't want them back, but I did wonder.

I walked towards the door, and the girls were there, all standing close and ready to help.

"Can I have a few more minutes? I want to see Cross," I said.

"Of course," Dakota said.

"Just don't do anything stupid," Paris said.

I smiled again, but I knew it likely looked forced. "Of course," I echoed.

The girls led me down the hall to the right where the

Bradys were sitting, all in various states of pacing or worry.

They looked up at me when I got there, and I held back a flinch.

I didn't want to see their anger or their pain.

Arden spoke first.

"They've already let us all in to see them," Arden said quickly. "But there's still some time that you can go in if you want."

"Yes, I need to see him," I whispered, my voice shaky.

"Of course. Our parents are on their way, they're just catching a flight," she said, rambling.

I looked at the others in the room, the man who had to be Arden's husband, the other two that looked like Cross, who were probably Nate and Prior. But I wasn't really focusing on them. I needed to keep moving.

I heard Nate draw in a breath, and I looked over my shoulder to see him staring at Myra. But then he turned, and so did she. I didn't have the brainpower to focus on what was happening.

I just kept moving, had to keep going.

Another nurse and Arden led me to one of the rooms, and I nodded and smiled as we walked, and they talked, but I wasn't really listening.

"Macon is next door. They're both going to be fine," Arden whispered.

And then her husband was there, holding his wife as tears slid down her cheeks. I still couldn't cry. I couldn't do much of anything.

Instead, I walked in and saw Cross lying on the bed, his eyes closed, his breathing deep as monitors beeped, and his IV pumped fluids into his body.

I didn't even know the details about what had happened or what kind of surgery he'd had.

I've been too focused on my issues and the cops and trying to get out so I could be alone, that I didn't know much of anything.

I usually loved to have the details. I needed that.

"You're staring," a gruff voice said from the bed, and I froze.

"Cross," I whispered. This time, a single tear did slide down my cheek. Damn it.

"Hey," he whispered. "You're safe."

"You...you're here. Macon is here. I'm...It's my fault," I muttered.

"If I could get out of this bed, I'd hug you and tell you it isn't. Don't you dare fucking blame yourself for this."

"But it *is* my fault," I whispered. "I'm sorry you're hurt because of me. Your brother almost died because of me. Chris *is* dead because of me."

"Chris is dead because of his choices," Cross growled.

"And Macon is going to be fine." I saw the relief on his face, and I almost died again inside.

My fault. All this is my fault.

"When I get out of this bed, we'll talk through it. We'll deal with it together. You and me, Hazel. We've got this."

It was like he was stabbing me with each word, broken shards of the person I wanted to be slicing into my skin. Into my soul.

I shook my head and wrapped my arms around my body.

"I can't, Cross."

His eyes narrowed. "You can't, or you won't?"

"I don't know what the difference is anymore. But this *is* my fault. And I don't know how to fix this. I'm sorry. You have your family, and they'll take good care of you. But I'm the reason you're lying there. I'm the reason all of this happened. And...I need to think about that. I need time. Please give me time to think. Please. I'm sorry. I'm so sorry." Before he could say anything, before he could even reach out to me, I rocked on my feet, pivoting as fast as I could since I was still hurting, and then walked quickly out of his room. My name on his lips was the last thing I heard as I moved past the others and made my way into the waiting room.

Everyone stared at me, but I went straight to Paris and

took her hand. She gave me a surprised look, and I squeezed. "I need to go home," I whispered.

She searched my face, and the others came with me, leaving the Bradys behind.

Leaving Cross where he lay.

I didn't deserve him. I didn't deserve any of them.

As I broke inside, and the others kept silent, I wondered how I was going to fix this. Was there any fixing this?

Maybe Thomas had won in the end. He had broken me. I wasn't his, but I wasn't my own woman anymore either.

I didn't know who I was, and I couldn't be with Cross until I figured that out.

Or maybe ever.

Chapter 20

CROSS

TWO WEEKS. TWO WEEKS OF DOCTOR APPOINTMENTS and healing and cursing and changing bandages. But now I was home. And alone.

Well, not completely alone. My brothers each took shifts at the house, along with my sister and some of the Montgomerys. At first, they had wanted to put Macon and me in the same house so we could heal together, but both of us had wanted to be in our own homes to heal where we could feel a bit normal. At least, as normal as you could be with two of five family members getting shot in a twenty-minute period.

Macon wasn't really talking to me, and I didn't know how I felt about that. We needed to talk about what was wrong, but I knew I wasn't in any place to figure that out yet.

And I was stewing in my own blame, trying to figure out how I could have been so wrong about Chris.

I knew Hazel blamed herself, there was no denying that.

I had to figure out how to fix this.

Needed to make this better.

I knew she was in pain, but there was nothing I could do about it when I was still stuck at home, trying to heal from wounds that took time. I wanted her by my side, but I knew she was scared, and I didn't want to stress her out. I'd fallen for her, but I didn't know how she felt about me.

I would never forget seeing her lying there, trying to save herself, struggling to get out of her restraints.

I could never un-hear the sounds of her screams, never un-see the look on her face when she stood there, gun in hand, a dead man at her feet.

I would have done anything to save her from the actions she had been forced to take because of a man hell-bent on having her.

I just hadn't realized that the man I had trusted with half of my business, the guy I had called my friend, would also end up being so cruel.

My hands shook. and I shifted on the couch a bit, careful of my tender new skin and wound.

I was doing fine, healing like I should. While physical therapy was a bitch, I was doing well. So was Macon.

But none of us were really talking about the fact that we had almost died. It was like it was too difficult to even contemplate putting those words together to form a sentence.

Add to that the fact that Hazel wasn't here, and I had no idea what the fuck I was doing.

I loved her. I fucking loved her, but I couldn't help her.

I had called her once. She hadn't answered, so I hadn't called again.

Maybe that was on me. Perhaps I should have pushed, but I knew she needed space. She had told me so herself.

I also knew the women in her life wouldn't leave her alone completely.

So she wasn't sitting alone, trying to contemplate what she was going to do. The fact that Arden had told me that the girls were watching her gave me some solace.

At least she wasn't completely alone.

But then again, neither was I. Today, I was, since I was on a break between shifts of the Bradys and Mont-gomerys. I had no one else around.

It was just me, sitting and trying to figure out what the fuck to do.

I really wasn't good at contemplating my life.

My business had burned to the ground, and there would be inquiries about that—beyond Chris and what he had done that night. And that was fine, it gave me time to think.

The pieces inside the shop that had burned hadn't been those for commission, they were ones I had made for myself. It hurt to lose them, but I had already moved my paperwork, files, and the important pieces to my home studio.

I'd had to answer to the cops about that, but when I'd explained about Chris and all of the financial audits we were about to go through, they understood.

Plus, there had been evidence of what Chris had done with the business, the building, and what had happened after, as well as the fact that Macon and Hazel had spoken up.

No one thought I had anything to do with the fire, other than the fact that I had really bad decision-making skills when it came to choosing business partners.

And that was that. Chris Cross Furniture was done, and though I had enough money to last me a good long while, I needed to figure out what to do.

I wanted to continue making furniture, but maybe it would just be as Cross Furniture.

Or maybe I would find something else to do with art.

I didn't know, but I had some time to figure it out. In fact, all I had these days was time.

I couldn't do much of anything but sit here and twiddle my thumbs, trying to figure out what the fuck I was going to do with my life.

And what the hell I was going to do about Hazel.

I loved her. I wanted to be with her. I'd given her space like she'd asked. I wouldn't force myself into her vicinity like Thomas had, but I needed to see her. I had to hold her, to make sure she was there, whole, and the woman I had fallen for.

As soon as I was healed enough, I would go to her. We'd had enough space. We needed to talk this out. Even if it ended—and it just might if that's what she wanted—I needed to have my say, as well.

I needed to tell her how I felt. And she needed to listen. If, in the end, I still had to walk away, I would.

But I didn't want to.

All I wanted was her.

If I had her, maybe I could figure out what I needed to do. Who I needed to be.

The doorbell rang, and I winced before trying to get

up until someone put their key in the lock, and I knew I wasn't alone.

Prior walked in, dark shadows under his eyes. He sat down, shaking his head.

"Long day?" I asked.

"The longest. But I'm not going to bore you with all of that. We'll talk about it later."

"Oh?"

"We can talk about it."

"Not right now. I'm trying to get through it. Anyway, I'm here to talk about you. What's going on with you?"

I held up my arms and gestured around my empty home. "I have no job, no prospects, no woman, and I'm healing from a gunshot wound. I'm doing great."

Prior winced. "Sorry, I just don't know what to say. Like, how the fuck is this happening to our family?" he asked.

"Mom and Dad asked that almost every day the full week that they were here," I said dryly.

Prior just shook his head and smiled. It was good to see him smile; he didn't do much of that these days given his job.

Our parents had come to take care of Macon and me but had gone home after a week, even though they'd wanted to stay longer.

But with so many of us, they knew they could leave

and come back. We could take care of ourselves. They'd said they would be back in a month to stay for another week.

While it had been good to see them, I was glad to have some time alone to think.

Even though that might not be the best thing for me right now.

"What are you going to do about Hazel?" Prior asked, and my eyes widened.

"I'm going to go to her. I gave her some time, but now it's time for us to talk it out and figure out what the fuck we're doing."

"And if she tells you she doesn't want to see you again?" Prior asked.

My gut churned, and my jaw tightened. "Then I'll go. But I was a little drugged when I let her walk away before, not to mention that I was strapped to the bed and an IV. I had to just let her walk away. And I know we both have a lot of shit to deal with now, fuck, all of us do, her friends and our family included. And we'll deal with it. But we need to talk it out. Together. I can't just walk away because it's easier. Even if it seems like it could be easier."

Prior searched my face and gave me a tight nod. "Good. She's good for you. I know she probably blames herself for what happened, but that was all on that asshole. Both assholes. But Chris wasn't a murderer. And we both know that."

I nodded, swallowing hard. "He just made some really bad fucking decisions."

"Sadly, he paid the price with his life," Prior said. "That's something we'll all have to deal with for a long fucking time. But we will. For now, however, I'm going to make you dinner, even though I'm not as good a cook as Arden or you. Then we'll eat and pretend that everything is fine, and you can tell me exactly how you're going to get Hazel back."

"I don't have a plan," I whispered.

"Then it's a good thing I'm here."

"When's the last time you had a serious relationship?" I asked.

"I haven't. Not really. So I guess I'll learn from you while I try to teach you. It'll be a symbiotic relationship of what the fuck."

I laughed, wincing a bit at the pain in my side.

I knew I wasn't going to let Hazel go, not without talking first.

I still had nightmares, picturing what had been done to her, the pain we'd both had to endure. That was something I would have to deal with for the rest of my life.

But I wasn't going to let myself wallow in solitude and

misery when I knew that I loved her, and I needed to tell her as much.

If she said she didn't love me and wanted nothing to do with me, I'd figure out how to live with that.

But until then, I had to bare my soul to her.

I just didn't know how to fucking do that.

How did I even start?

Chapter 21

HAZEL

I STOOD AT MY FRONT DOOR, MY HANDS SHAKING, BUT it was fine. I knew what I was doing. I could do this.

I needed to talk with Cross. I needed to ask him to forgive me.

Not just for what had happened at the cabin, or even for all the pain and blood. For how I left.

Nobody deserved to be lying in a hospital bed, only to be left behind.

It was callous, thoughtless, but I had been so in my head, I'd stood in my own way.

I hadn't been thinking, not really. Hadn't been able to

get through my own fears and pain and trauma. And in the end, I'd left him.

And I couldn't forgive myself for that. Now I had to beg him for forgiveness.

I let out a breath. I knew I could do this. I just needed to go to Cross's home and beg.

Maybe even beg him to love me.

But that might be going too far.

The doorbell rang, and I let out a little scream.

Someone slammed their hand on the door, and I clutched my hands into fists at my sides.

"Hazel? Did you scream?"

Cross. Cross was here.

I let out a shaky laugh then looked through the peephole. There it was, his beautiful, bearded face. I almost cried.

Instead, I flipped all the locks, opened the door, and looked at him.

He looked healthy, and he wasn't falling down.

He wasn't covered in blood or attached to tubes or lying down, weak.

All the images that I had relived every single night for the past two weeks slammed into my mind again, and I simply tried to breathe.

It was hard to do when all I wanted to do was hold him and tell him that I was sorry and that I hoped he was doing well.

But I didn't know how to say all that.

"Cross," I whispered.

"Are you okay? What happened?"

"I was just standing by the door, and you rang the doorbell, and it startled me. I was trying to get up the courage to come and see you, and now you're here, and I screamed like an idiot."

Cross ran a hand over his face and then smiled, the relief in his eyes hitting me hard.

"Jesus. I thought you were hurt again. Hell. Can I hold you? Is that too much to ask? Because I really need to fucking hold you right now."

We needed to talk, I knew that. We needed to do a lot of things besides falling into each other, but I didn't care right now.

Instead, I wrapped my arms around his waist, careful of where he'd been shot, the spot that meant he'd almost died, and simply held him. His arms slid around me, and he pulled me close. I inhaled his masculine scent, the woodsy one that always made me shiver.

"You're here," I whispered.

"I am, Hazel. Fuck. That scream just now... I never want to hear it again. Holy hell. It's already in my nightmares from the cabin, and hearing it again? Fuck."

"I startle easily. I'm working on it. Cross. Am I hurting you?"

"No, you're not touching the wound. But you already knew that. You know exactly where it is."

I was talking to his chest while holding him, inhaling his scent. I never wanted to let go.

I just wanted to hold him.

"I can't believe I almost lost you."

"I was thinking the same fucking thing."

"Come in, let's talk."

"Let me just hold you."

And then I heard him inhale, and I sank into him, just holding him for a little bit longer.

I wasn't sure how long we stood there before he finally let me go but gripped my hands.

"Invite me inside?"

I already had, but I did so again. Then, we were both inside, and I was locking the door behind me like I always did, knowing he was watching me, making sure every single deadbolt was locked.

"I'm glad you're still doing that," he whispered.

"It doesn't make me neurotic or paranoid?" I asked.

"My brothers and brother-in-law helped me put more locks on my door. I think we're all going to be a little paranoid and neurotic for a while. But that's fine. Because fuck, Hazel. I almost lost you, and I don't know what I would have done if I had."

"I need to tell you that I'm sorry."

Anger flashed in his gaze, and I winced.

"You better not be sorry for what happened."

"I can be sorry you were involved in it, even though I know it wasn't my fault. That *was* what was running through my head during your hospital stay, and it's why I acted the way I did. But I was just going through the motions. I wasn't thinking clearly. Now, though, I want to say I'm sorry for leaving like I did. I shouldn't have done that. I should have waited and tried to think it through, talk to you. But I didn't know the words were coming out of my mouth that day until they were said. I hurt you. Hurt you more than going through surgery and being shot. And I'm not sure I can ever forgive myself for that."

Cross cursed again, but I didn't flinch. I loved the sound of his voice. I loved that he was here. I loved *him*.

"I kept thinking about what I would have done had the situation been reversed."

My breath caught at his words, and hope flared. I tamped it down. I was still afraid to hope.

"Only...Hazel? Please, just never do that again. Never leave me. I know I probably sound like Thomas right now. I need to stop."

My eyes widened, and I moved forward, putting my hands on his chest. "No. That's not the things Thomas said. He told me to never leave him because I was his possession. I've had years of therapy to get through that. But I'm not your possession, just like you're not mine. However, I want to be yours in a way. I never should have left. I shouldn't have walked away when things got tough. But I was scared of what I was feeling, what had happened, and I wasn't thinking properly. I *was* on my way to you. I swear. I was going to fall to my knees and beg you for forgiveness. Because I love you, Cross Brady. I love you so much. I never thought I could love like this. What I had with Thomas before? That wasn't love. It was a one-sided infatuation that I told myself was love, and it got twisted into something horrible."

"Hazel," Cross whispered.

I shook my head, cutting him off. "No, let me finish. I love you to the depths of my soul. You make me smile and laugh. You make me think. You make me feel like I can do anything. I walked away because I blamed myself for what happened. If you can't forgive me for that, I'll understand. But I want you to know that I'll never do it again. I'll never walk away when things get hard or if I blame myself. I'll talk to you. I'll just try not to have a slight concussion when that happens."

I laughed softly when he did, knowing that I was rambling.

"Can I touch you?" he whispered, and I nodded. He slid his hands through my hair, and I remembered that I had cut it since I had last seen him.

"I like it shorter. I like it long, too. I just like you."

"I had to cut it...after."

"I know. Arden mentioned it."

"I like that she's the go-between. But I'd rather we not need one."

"I get you. And I love you, too, Hazel." My heart stopped. "I love you so fucking much. I was coming here to make sure that you knew that. I gave you space because you asked for it, but I was coming to see if you still needed that. I don't want to fucking go. And I'm sorry, too. I'm sorry that everything happened, but we went through that together, and we can go through this together, too. I'm just so fucking sorry that any of it happened at all."

Tears were freely streaming down my cheeks now, and I leaned forward, kissing his bearded chin. He looked down and then kissed me softly, his lips parted just a bit.

I swiped my tongue over his and moaned. I'd missed him.

"I'm so fucking happy I sat down at that table."

I looked at him, crying even more. "And I love that you were my accidental date, even if I know that, in the end, there was nothing accidental about it."

Then his lips were on mine, and I was smiling, breathing him in.

I knew we had more to go through, things to talk about, and worries to process. And we would.

But there would be no more walking away from each other. Because we could do this, as long as we did it together.

I had been wrong in thinking I could go it alone. Wrong in thinking I needed to.

He had beaten me to the punch, but I would grovel until the end of my days so he knew what I felt.

As he held me, and as I cried in his arms, I knew I never needed to be alone again.

I had found my forever, one I hadn't even known I needed.

They say that you find forever only once, and while I had thought I'd found it before, I knew now that I was wrong.

I had found my forever in Cross, and I was never giving it away. Never returning it.

He was my forever.

Epilogue

CROSS

LATER

I licked up Hazel's inner thigh. I loved the way she shivered for me.

She moaned, her legs around my neck as her hands covered her breasts, her back arching as she lay on our bed.

I hummed along her clit, eating and tasting and wanting more.

She was swollen from our lovemaking earlier, and all I wanted to do was indulge, to feast, to lick and taste until the day ended. But it was still morning, and we had some-place to be. I had to be quick about it.

"We're going to be late," she whispered.

"Then I'll go faster," I said, loving that her mind always followed the same path as mine. At least, usually.

I licked again, speared her with two fingers, and hummed on her clit once more. When she arched against me, her whole body shaking, my name on her lips, I moved over her, sheathing myself in her tight heat as she shuddered. My lips were on hers, and she moaned, her fingernails raking my back. We moved as one, our bodies arcing, sweat-slick, and needy.

When I rolled over onto my back, she rode me, my hands on her breasts once more, then her hips, her face. She moved, taking control, her whole body one sensuous movement, all touch and need.

I couldn't breathe, couldn't focus, all I wanted was her. When my balls tightened, and I came, she came with me, both of us shaking and completely sated.

We had ditched condoms about a month ago after we finished our testing, and I was finally cleared by my doctors to have as much sex as we wanted. Thank the gods for PT.

I slowly slid out of her, kissed her softly, and then both of us went to clean up.

After all, we were having a very large party at our

house later in the afternoon, so the place had to look right, and I couldn't walk around naked—not when my family would be here soon.

"I'm not showering with you," Hazel said, and I smiled.

"It's like you read my mind. I hadn't even asked you yet."

"Still not doing it."

"Why? We have so much fun in the shower."

"No, we waste water. And although you have that lovely bench in there, so it makes for great angles, we are going to be late. Now you're making me sound like the rabbit from *Alice in Wonderland*."

"Maybe. But you're a very cute rabbit."

"You already got some. Twice this morning, and three times last night. We all know that you're virile. I'm going to shower in the guest bathroom, and you are going to meet me in the kitchen later to get ready for our day."

I shook my head and quickly showered as she walked away.

She had moved in with me the week before, and we were still figuring things out. She was spending so many hours and nights at my house already, it just made sense.

And today was the celebration of our cohabitation.

We would put her house on the market shortly, and one day soon, I would propose to her. We were still working up to that, but after everything we had gone through, it made sense that we never wanted to spend a night alone again.

I never wanted to be without her, so that was just fine by me.

I had already purchased her ring so I could propose, but I didn't want to move too fast. The way we had moved so quickly already might be too much for some, but it worked for us. When the time was right, I would pop the question. Hopefully, I'd have her family's blessing when I did—her family being Paris, Dakota, and Myra. And that was just fine with me. I thought they liked me, so hopefully, they'd let me marry their best friend.

After all, it was a damn good way to finish Hazel's part of their dating plan.

I knew everybody was waiting to start the next phase of their pact, with Paris coming up next. I was very interested to see how that went.

I quickly got dressed and headed to the kitchen to start setting up. It would take Hazel a bit longer to finish her hair, but I didn't mind. My woman had already made a checklist of what we needed out, and what needed to be prepped for the party.

I had just started setting up the food and making sure the place was clean when Hazel walked out, her hair done, a bright, satisfied smile on her face.

I had done that. No, check that, *we* had done that. And after everything that she had been through? It was my favorite fucking thing to see in the world.

"You look edible," I whispered. She leaned back, her hands outstretched.

"Don't. If you kiss me, we're going to have sex in the kitchen again, and it'll take a lot of cleaning to get it ready for the party. I won't be a part of that."

I threw my head back and laughed, suddenly saved by the doorbell.

"Let's get this party started." She clapped her hands together and gave me a wide smile. "I can't believe we're having a housewarming party already. It feels like I just moved in."

I leaned forward and kissed her on the lips. "You did just move in. Hence the party. Now, let's go see our family."

Everybody showed up almost at the same time, each bringing food of their own, as well as drinks and little presents.

Joshua, Dakota's son, came in, a potted plant in his hands, very carefully setting it on the floor.

"Mom let me bring it in, but I had to be really careful," Joshua said.

I leaned down and nodded solemnly. "You did a fine job."

"Your brother Macon helped me get it out of the car, but then I took it the rest of the way. I like Macon."

I smiled and reached out to squeeze the kid's shoulder. "I like Macon, too."

Macon wasn't exactly the same as he had been, though. While my brother had always been quiet and a little growly, he was also the one with a quick smile, just like Prior. He didn't smile as much anymore, and he didn't talk about it. I hoped that one day he would. But until then, we would all watch and be there for him.

Dakota was all of a sudden there, by Macon's side, taking the rest of her containers from him. Macon didn't say a word, just stared at her intently before going to the living room where Nate and Myra were glaring at each other. I had no idea why they were doing that, but when the group of us were together, it was always very interesting.

"You didn't have to make anything," I said.

"She always likes to make things, but she makes the best things, so I really want to know what's inside," Hazel said, taking a couple of containers from Dakota while I took the rest.

"Thank you," I said at the same time Hazel did, and we smiled at each other while Dakota rolled her eyes.

"You guys are so cute it's disgusting. However, I have adorable cupcakes with fillings that I hope you love. And I can't wait to see your house. Thank you for this."

"Seriously, the place looks great," Paris said. I like that you guys blended your lives. And who knew a date that I helped set up would end up so amazing?" Paris said, and Prior snorted from her side.

"Excuse me? Do you have something to say?" she asked.

"We all know that it had nothing to do with you. And everything to do with them. But sure, take the credit."

"Wow. I can't believe you just said that."

"What, the truth?"

The two started bickering, and Hazel and I looked at each other before walking away.

"It seems that our families are getting along just fine," Hazel said, wincing.

"We'll figure it out. At least, I hope so." I set down the cupcakes and then kissed Hazel again, holding her to me.

Arden and Liam arrived, pulling Prior and Paris away from each other.

It seemed that everybody got along but had their own odd quirks with one another. That didn't bother me because my family had their own quirks.

But as I held Hazel against my side, I couldn't help but think about exactly how we had gotten here, and what might come next.

Because, somehow, I had gotten more than I'd ever bargained for.

I had the woman of my dreams, a family I loved, and somehow, I was making it all work.

I had opened up a new shop, one bearing just my name, and I was still making a career out of something I loved.

This was a life I had never dreamed of for myself. Yet, somehow, I had been blessed with it.

I had been blessed with *her*.

And though no one had truly healed after what had happened, we were all moving on.

We had lost parts of ourselves that night when the blood had coated the floor, but we had found other parts.

I had to trust that that would be enough. That *we* would be enough.

Because the woman at my side was someone I wanted to be with for the rest of my life. Forever.

And as I looked at our families surrounding us, I knew that this was the life we had always been meant for, even if we hadn't thought it possible or planned for it.

For someone who was never good with words or emotions, I couldn't help but feel like maybe having it all happen accidentally was the only way it could have happened.

Sitting down at that table across from a beautiful woman with sad eyes was the happiest accident ever.

THE END
Next in the Promise Me series?
Prior & Paris take a turn in FROM THAT MOMENT

WANT TO READ A SPECIAL BONUS EPILOGUE FEATURING HAZEL & CROSS? CLICK HERE!

A Note from Carrie Ann Ryan

Thank you so much for reading **FOREVER ONLY ONCE.** I do hope if you liked this story, that you would please leave a review! Reviews help authors *and* readers.

The Brady Brothers and the Pact Sisters are so much fun. Just don't tell them that I've give them group names LOL.

Hazel and Cross went through a horrible ordeal, and yet found an HEA that made me cry and smile. And they are just the start!

Up next is Paris and Prior, an office romance turned dangerous. The other couples will be getting their HEAs as well!

And in case you missed it, Arden and Liam might be familiar if you read Wrapped in Ink!

And if you're new to my books, you can start

anywhere within the my interconnected series and catch up! Each book is a stand alone, so jump around!

Don't miss out on the Montgomery Ink World!

- Montgomery Ink (The Denver Montgomerys)
- Montgomery Ink: Colorado Springs (The Colorado Springs Montgomery Cousins)
- Montgomery Ink: Boulder (The Boulder Montgomery Cousins)
- Gallagher Brothers (Jake's Brothers from Ink Enduring)
- Whiskey and Lies (Tabby's Brothers from Ink Exposed)
- Fractured Connections (Mace's sisters from Fallen Ink)
- Less Than (Dimitri's siblings from Restless Ink)
- Promise Me (Arden's siblings from Wrapped in Ink)

If you want to make sure you know what's coming next from me, you can sign up for my newsletter at www. CarrieAnnRyan.com; follow me on twitter at @CarrieAnnRyan, or like my Facebook page. I also have a Facebook Fan Club where we have trivia, chats, and other goodies.

You guys are the reason I get to do what I do and I thank you.

Make sure you're signed up for my MAILING LIST so you can know when the next releases are available as well as find giveaways and FREE READS.

Happy Reading!

The Promise Me Series:
>Book 1: Forever Only Once
>Book 2: From That Moment
>Book 3: Far From Destined
>Book 4: From Our First

WANT TO READ A SPECIAL **BONUS EPILOGUE** FEATURING HAZEL & CROSS? **CLICK HERE!**

Want to keep up to date with the next Carrie Ann Ryan Release? Receive Text Alerts easily!
Text CARRIE to 210-741-8720

About the Author

Carrie Ann Ryan is the New York Times and USA Today bestselling author of contemporary, paranormal, and young adult romance. Her works include the Montgomery Ink, Redwood Pack, Fractured Connections, and Elements of Five series, which have sold over 3.0 million books worldwide. She started writing while in graduate school for her advanced degree in chemistry and hasn't stopped since. Carrie Ann has written over seventy-five novels and novellas with more in the works. When she's not losing herself in her emotional and action-packed worlds, she's reading as much as she can while wrangling her clowder of cats who have more followers than she does.

www.CarrieAnnRyan.com

Also from Carrie Ann Ryan

The Montgomery Ink: Boulder Series:

Book 1: Wrapped in Ink

Book 2: Sated in Ink

Book 3: Embraced in Ink

Book 4: Seduced in Ink

Book 4.5: Captured in Ink

The Montgomery Ink: Fort Collins Series:

Book 1: Inked Persuasion

The Less Than Series:

Book 1: Breathless With Her

Book 2: Reckless With You

Book 3: Shameless With Him

The Elements of Five Series:

Book 1: From Breath and Ruin

Book 2: From Flame and Ash

Book 3: From Spirit and Binding

The Promise Me Series:

Book 1: Forever Only Once

Book 2: From That Moment

Book 3: Far From Destined

Book 4: From Our First

The Fractured Connections Series:

Book 1: Breaking Without You

Book 2: Shouldn't Have You

Book 3: Falling With You

Book 4: Taken With You

Montgomery Ink: Colorado Springs

Book 1: Fallen Ink

Book 2: Restless Ink

Book 2.5: Ashes to Ink

Book 3: Jagged Ink

Book 3.5: Ink by Numbers

Montgomery Ink:

Book 0.5: Ink Inspired

Book 0.6: Ink Reunited

Book 1: Delicate Ink

Book 1.5: Forever Ink

Book 2: Tempting Boundaries

Book 3: Harder than Words

Book 4: Written in Ink

Book 4.5: Hidden Ink

Book 5: Ink Enduring

Book 6: Ink Exposed

Book 6.5: Adoring Ink

Book 6.6: Love, Honor, & Ink

Book 7: Inked Expressions

Book 7.3: Dropout

Book 7.5: Executive Ink

Book 8: Inked Memories

Book 8.5: Inked Nights

Book 8.7: Second Chance Ink

The Gallagher Brothers Series:

Book 1: Love Restored

Book 2: Passion Restored

Book 3: Hope Restored

The Whiskey and Lies Series:

Book 1: Whiskey Secrets

Book 2: Whiskey Reveals

Also from Carrie Ann Ryan

Book 7.7: The Hunted Heart

Book 8: Wicked Wolf

The Branded Pack Series:
(Written with Alexandra Ivy)

Book 1: Stolen and Forgiven

Book 2: Abandoned and Unseen

Book 3: Buried and Shadowed

Dante's Circle Series:

Book 1: Dust of My Wings

Book 2: Her Warriors' Three Wishes

Book 3: An Unlucky Moon

Book 3.5: His Choice

Book 4: Tangled Innocence

Book 5: Fierce Enchantment

Book 6: An Immortal's Song

Book 7: Prowled Darkness

Book 8: Dante's Circle Reborn

Holiday, Montana Series:

Book 1: Charmed Spirits

Book 2: Santa's Executive

Book 3: Finding Abigail

Book 4: Her Lucky Love

Book 5: Dreams of Ivory

Also from Carrie Ann Ryan

The Happy Ever After Series:
Flame and Ink
Ink Ever After

Single Title:
Finally Found You

Made in the USA
Columbia, SC
22 June 2020